CONSTRICTOR

JOHN LEE SCHNEIDER

SEVEREDPRESS

CONSTRICTOR

ISBN: 978-1-923165-27-4

"Trust in me. Just in me. Shut your eyes. And trust in me."

Kaa the Python
The Jungle Book, 1967

CHAPTER 1

Buffy was a python. She was a pet. Frank had raised her from a hatchling. He bought her from a black-market dealer overseas, and smuggled her into the United States himself.

Frank had been in the military at the time, coming home from completing his final tour – he probably could have been court-marshaled if they'd caught him.

During his active service, he'd been based at Fort Collins in northern Colorado, and in the years since his discharge, he'd mostly been living in the Boulder area. Just recently, he'd moved into a small apartment just outside of town, along Interstate 25 on the way to Denver.

His exit was a gas-station stop, with a small grocery-market and motel. There were a few houses patched on the hill behind the overpass. Frank's apartment building was tucked out of sight, in a little wooded area, down the little access-road barely half-a-mile from the highway.

Frank had only been there a few months, but despite his efforts to keep a low-profile, he tended to be a known figure wherever he lived. He was mid-sized but cut a whipcord, weaponized figure – military sharp under affected civilian shabbiness.

"Where were you deployed?" was always the question Frank got first.

"Wherever somebody needed shootin'," was always his reply.

In conversation, Frank was quick to smile or laugh, and his neighbors, past and present, knew him as friendly and helpful – the type known to carry grocery bags, or do handyman-work for the old lady next door.

But over the years, not many of his neighbors ever knew about Buffy – although, those that did, knew he was quite proud of her.

During the brief period Frank attended college post-service, living on campus, one of his neighbors, a young co-ed, recalled him asking if he'd watch his snake for a few days while he was out of town. Frank had brought the young lady over to watch him feed Buffy a live rabbit, and she described how the snake reacted instantaneously, coiling the unfortunate hare in half-a-second – squeezing its heart stopped in less than a minute, but keeping the little creature wrapped for several minutes, making sure it was dead, before it began to swallow.

Aghast, the young co-ed had declined snake-sitting duties. That had been when Buffy was barely twelve-feet long.

She was now over twenty-four-feet.

Reticulated pythons – *Python reticulatus* – were the largest snakes in the world, with many reported at twenty-feet or more. But Frank was pretty sure Buffy was a record-breaker for captive snakes.

There were greater lengths than twenty-four-feet recorded, but not with any greater evidence than the pen and ink that said so back in the 1940s or 50s. What records like that actually reflected was the irresistible exaggeration that invariably swung the scales with giant snakes. Frank was pretty sure there were never any sixty-foot anacondas – or even any thirty-footers. There weren't even any thirty-foot pythons, which were more slender and elongated.

A long-standing record reported by Guinness, a twenty-eight-foot giant named *Cassius*, was simply not that big – its preserved skeleton was just over twenty-feet. A cash-reward offered by the Nature Society, up to fifty-thousand dollars, for a live thirty-foot python, has never been collected.

By 'scientific' record – that is to say, a dead or anesthetized snake, measured by or in the presence of a scientist – the largest retics were around twenty-one-feet.

There *was*, however, solid practical evidence of twenty-three and twenty-four-footers in captivity today – documented on camera, if not the literature.

And documented or not, Frank had the proof of a twenty-four-footer right in front of him. He'd measured her himself, taking her out in the woods, letting her crawl around, and stretched her out between two pegs.

He had also weighed her on an industrial scale, where she had topped out at over three-hundred pounds. And that had been a couple of years ago – she'd grown since then, in both length and bulk.

That was another asterisk the scientific community always added, suggesting that captive snakes, typically heavier than in the wild, were obese.

Frank would suggest it was more a case of living optimally – being able to eat when actually hungry, as opposed to prowling around the jungle, sometimes for days or weeks, before it was actually able to catch something.

This was an animal built to fast if it had to, but a twenty-three-foot python, emaciated at two-hundred pounds, after starving for three-months living in the wild, was no more 'natural' than the well-fed snake that weighed three-hundred.

But despite her size, it was remarkable the compact space Buffy lived in within the confines of Frank's small one-bedroom apartment. She actually occupied the bedroom – her terrarium was four-feet high, and five-by-ten-feet wide – half of it was a pool with a constantly-operating pump, that both moderated her temperature, and kept the tank clean of waste. There was also a six-inch steel bar splitting the middle, mimicking an overhanging tree branch.

Buffy got the bedroom partly because of space issues, leaving Frank to sleep on his fold-out sofa in the living room. That wasn't a big deal – he was used to roughing it in the military, and used to sleeping on the couch during his marriage.

Of course, it was also prudent to keep the terrarium out of sight. Buffy was, after all, an illegal animal, and a potentially dangerous one.

He had been called foolish just for owning such a creature – just as he had been called foolish for joining the military.

But Frank believed danger was always related to personal behavior.

Buffy represented very basic instincts. She responded favorably to positive stimuli – Frank often petted and massaged her, peeling her loose skin – generally grooming and pampering her, and therefore she was receptive to his presence and accepting to his touch when he would sometimes pull her out of her cage, and let her lounge around on the floor.

That practice was a bit iffy, Frank knew – handling a snake Buffy's size alone in a tight space was inherently dangerous. On the other hand, he lived with her, and the whole point of conditioning was not to create the impression of being prey. That, and keeping her generally comfortable and happy. And getting out of her cage once in a while left her less cranky.

And Buffy *could* get cranky. If you caught her at the wrong moment, suddenly you might find yourself dealing with one of the most efficient killing and eating machines on the planet.

Reticulated pythons were an aggressive species, prone to bite first – they took on threats aggressively and instantaneously.

That had led to a little friction with Frank's wife.

Barb had the typical girl-reaction the first time this charming ex-soldier had brought her home to his place.

Pleasantly sudsed-up from a night out drinking and dancing at one of the local bars favored by GI's and the girls who liked them, Barb had blinked back almost sober when her eyes focused first on the ten-foot glass enclosure, and then what was inside it.

Buffy had popped up interestedly, eyeing her speculatively.

"Is it *looking* at me?" Barb asked – the snake's eyes were yellow, and unblinking – staring – a little too happy to see you.

Frank had smiled deviously.

"She's probably deciding if you're something I brought home for her as a treat."

With those eager yellow eyes riveted on her, Barb had suddenly been creeped out.

"That's not funny," she said, in a moment of temper, and turned for the door.

Frank had grabbed her and pulled her back, spinning her into his strong arms like circling coils.

"Don't worry," he said, dipping her back, "I brought you home for *my* treat."

Then he had kissed her – a deep, full-bodied kiss – and she had relented.

They had married six-months later.

Buffy, however, continued to be a source of friction.

"I never got past those eyes," Barb confided to Frank later. "The way she looked at me that first time. Every time I walked in, it was the same thing. She perked every single time she saw me. She watched me every second I was there. And that look in her eyes never changed."

"That's the predator's eyes," Frank acknowledged. "Like she's happy to see you."

He smiled grimly. "But not in a *good* way."

That was something you could never forget, because, at the end of the day, Buffy was a very large predator, with a very small brain, that fed on human-sized prey.

There were many real-life accounts of pet constrictors, anything from Burmese to African rock pythons, killing people, including their owners. Although the victims of actual *predatory* attacks were usually children, adults were often killed, as well, if not necessarily eaten, because even smaller snakes can constrict. In October 2008, a twenty-five year-old woman was killed by a thirteen-foot pet python, and she was found dead with no apparent attempt by the snake to eat her.

Of course, there *were* real-life cases of giant snakes actually *swallowing* adult human beings, and these almost exclusively involved reticulated pythons.

Besides being large enough, retics in their native habitat are known to hunt Macaque monkeys – and in the manner that Great White sharks will target human surfers on the surface, because the shadow resembles a seal, the diminutive natives that populate the region are likewise regular targets of reticulated pythons. One-in-four members of the Indonesian *Aeta* tribe report surviving attacks by large pythons, and there are several confirmed accounts of adult humans being swallowed – one recorded on video by witnesses.

So, in fairness to Barb, being scared of Buffy was not an unreasonable fear to have. And to her credit, she had tried not to be *that* girlfriend/wife and make it into an issue.

She felt more uncomfortable, however, when Frank wasn't home to chaperone.

He often went camping – another interest Barb did not share. Moreover, she learned after the first time she went on one of these trips, that they were primarily old army-buddy drinking-binges, best left to him and his friends.

As a wife, Barb was content to let Frank '*howl at the moon*', as he phrased it, and get the wildness out of his system. Raucousing in the woods now and then, kept him out of the local bars, and Frank never drank when he was alone with her at home.

It was almost as if during these forest-trysts, Frank seemed to become a different person – embracing the primitive – returning to the barbaric war-face he must have worn during his combat-days. It was when he wore this face that Barb could see him shooting someone in cold blood.

He was, in fact, a trained-killer, Barb realized – it was a primitive and savage natural instinct, enhanced by intensive training, and practiced enough to get good at it.

Barb, for her part, was happy enough to let Frank go out in the woods, every so often, and work all that out on his own.

But that *did* leave her in the care of a twenty-four-foot constrictor.

Truthfully, it usually wasn't a bother. Buffy didn't really require feeding – at least not before Frank would typically be back. It was mostly just monitoring the temperature of the cage.

And of course, making sure it stayed locked.

That was the problem on the one day Buffy had gotten out while Barb had been home alone.

Frank had not been camping – he'd just buzzed up quickly to the store – a ten-minute jaunt.

But it was almost enough.

The latch on Buffy's cage had simply failed to lock. The cylinder inside had broken apart, but it wasn't obvious, when Frank last sealed the lid.

Barb would speculate later whether Buffy *knew* – the big snake didn't usually poke at the cage's lid when it was locked. But on this day, she had pushed the loose trapdoor open.

Frank had only been gone a few minutes, but Barb was in the house alone.

And Buffy had been watching her every minute for a long time now.

Barb was working in the kitchen when she turned to see Buffy reared-up out of her cage, already moving, her head like an arrow, those yellow eyes purposeful – ready to finally pounce.

Letting out a scream, Barb made a break for the door, but the snake's teeth snagged out and caught her leg, tripping her up, and she collapsed over a kitchen chair.

This was part of what saved her life, because Buffy initially wrapped her coils around Barb and the chair together.

Contrary to popular belief, constricting snakes did not kill by suffocation so much as compression. They were like an incredibly tight blood pressure-cuff that simply choked-off your circulation, including your heart.

And once circulation stops, brain-death occurs within seven to ten minutes – a faster death than produced by any venomous snake.

"It wasn't like the movies," Barb said later, "where you see victims wrestling with the coils. This was like being in a full-body sleeper-hold."

She had been wrapped less than a minute and was already losing consciousness when Frank arrived home.

With efficient movement, and that same grim, primitive face he wore in the woods, he quickly grabbed-up a bottle of whiskey out of the parlor, popping the seal. The next moment, he was over her, rolling her back to get at Buffy's head, and poured the liquor all over the big snake's mouth, where she gripped Barb's leg.

The response was immediate. Buffy released, letting go her teeth, dropping her coils, and seeming to shake her head at the foul taste, retreating like a sidewinder back to the safety of her cage.

Barb was not hurt beyond the fang marks that dotted her lower leg.

But that was still enough for her.

She had told Frank unequivocally, that if he didn't get rid of that snake, then she was leaving.

Frank had refused.

Barb had promptly reset – the ultimatum was changed to, "Get rid of that snake or *you're* leaving."

That one had stuck.

That was how Frank ended up in this little one-bedroom apartment on the outskirts of town.

'*Modest accommodations*' would be how the news reports described it after the story of the events that happened that spring eventually broke nationwide.

CHAPTER 2

They were 'modest accommodations' indeed.

The place was called 'The Glen', small and basic, although it was a nice-enough little complex. Circumstances notwithstanding, Frank had certainly lived in worse.

All six buildings were built bungalow-style, to accommodate the geography – three-apartment structures on each side of the steep drive, stair-stepping down the slope into the basin, totaling twelve individual living-units. Each building was a sort of duplex, sharing a partial back or side wall, but on split levels, due to the sharply sloping hillside.

Frank's apartment was at the very bottom of the drive – Room 12 – and under the property's previous owner, it had been the on-site maintenance man's reserved unit, and his door was directly opposite the main office, which was built across a small foot-bridge, over a man-made pond that surrounded the small building like a moat.

The complex itself was nestled down in the gully of a small wetlands area, alongside the arterial road that led out to Interstate 25. There were a couple of larger apartment complexes a few miles further on, along with a number of houses – it was not quite a neighborhood, with most of the area being undeveloped woodlands.

Down in the little gully was a mini-rainforest. The pond sported ducks, sometimes geese, as well as large carp – once pet goldfish, that had been released and were now grown huge and fat.

The neighbors were fairly typical. On the upper slope, were four post-college twenty-something couples, still in the living-together stage before marriage, and not yet hunting for a house. The apartments below had a couple of working-Joes, who Frank never saw, but knew they drove trucks, wore coveralls, and worked somewhere in the city. There were also a couple of middle-aged bachelors – one was Frank's immediate neighbor – although both of them were traveling salesman-types, living on the highway between Boulder and Denver, and they were home least of all.

Across the small lot, there was one of those little old ladies, who you always saw being led by a pair of those annoying little barking dogs, yanking at their leashes, biting at your ankles if you got close enough.

You could hear her out walking them, day and night. 'Eleanor' was her name, and she just *loved* Frank. She always stopped him to talk, invariably extending it into a chat – with her dogs yapping and snapping at his heels.

If you weren't careful, you could also get commissioned into doing the odd chore or project. On two occasions, Frank had gotten her old Cadillac started, unblocked her sink, and helped her install one of those security-screens that fit on the sliding glass doors on her back porch – so she could 'feel safe with the door open.'

Frank had to laugh. The screen attachment was literally built over mesh steel. For damn sure, no one was breaking through *that*. If it were him, he'd just go kick down the front door.

He didn't say anything to her, though – it was all about the old lady's peace of mind. The truth was, living in this oddball little nook was probably safer than almost anywhere in the city. Any nefarious characters would most likely be driving by on the highway.

Of course, he was less supportive of the little doggie-door she insisted he install in one corner. Not only did it invite the possibility of those damned nippy little dogs running freely in and out of the parking lot, always darting at your heels, the complex was also surrounded by woods – doggie-doors invited critters – raccoons, possum, and sometimes even coyotes.

Frank, of course, was also privy to a number of recent cases, cropping-up in the Florida Everglades, where people were actually discovering invasive *pythons* getting into their houses – but he didn't mention those.

But despite his objections, Eleanor was insistent, and Frank acquiesced – although he did solve part of the problem, by installing a lever-activated door, that could be locked from inside. The dogs could activate the mechanism by hitting the switch on either side, but it wouldn't open if it was locked, and would set off an alert-beep, like a doorbell, every time the door opened and closed.

That little feature went a long way towards keeping Eleanor's furry little ankle-biters from running loose, although the old lady was a tad bit neglectful about keeping it locked – both pooches had gotten out anyway, and Frank had a couple of torn pant legs to show for it.

A more congenial neighbor was Julia, who actually lived at the very top end of the complex, but as on-site manager, she spent most of her time down at the main office, and saw Frank on a daily basis.

Julia was in her early twenties, still in school, working on some total-bullshit-degree in something-or-other, and getting a break on rent by running the office. Frank knew the type – probably smart, but no doubt a bit of a bleeding heart.

She was a pretty one though. And even though she was quite a bit younger, she was obviously impressed with Frank. Ironically, he'd discovered a lot of these supposedly intellectual college girls really seemed to dig military-guys. Perhaps it was a bit of secret pleasure. Or maybe just a favorable comparison to fraternity slobs. In any case, Julia had been giving Frank 'those eyes', since the day he moved in.

Frank, who was somehow about to turn thirty-seven, had so far remained politely aloof.

Not that he was above trysting with the odd young hottie, but those were mostly the sort he met in strip-clubs. The age-gap seemed more apparent with a girl like Julia – she was a nice kid.

Emphasis on '*kid*'.

As he tried to explain it to one of his army buddies, there were girls you banged and couldn't care less – Julia wasn't one of those.

His friend, a certified dog named Rodney, had frowned, shaking his head.

"Never met one of those."

Of course, Julia was also the manager of the complex where he lived, and he had a twenty-four-foot python living illegally in his room.

Therefore, Frank decided it was best to keep Julia as just a friendly neighbor.

Besides, he was technically still married. Despite Barb's best efforts, she remained his wife. He'd consistently managed to lose all the papers he was supposed to sign.

Frank knew prospects for reconciliation were slim. He supposed he just had a hard time letting go.

And ultimately, despite his tough ex-military bearing, at heart, he was a softie who believed in the old love songs, and all the fairy-tales to go with it.

Of course, reality was never further away than his front window.

Apparently, just because every apartment complex had to have one, there was also the room with the loud neighbors. Sometimes it was because of parties. Other times it was fighting and domestic violence.

At The Glen, it was the latter. The woman who lived opposite Frank's place, sharing her wall with Eleanor, was a single mom, named Darcy. She had a six-year-old daughter, Lila. The boyfriend, in question, was Eddie.

Even more than Julia, Darcy had given Frank some serious eyes when he'd first moved in. She'd come knocking on his door, tarted-up, with clear intentions, and was a bit put-out when Frank declined to invite her in.

Frank knew the type and probably would have sent her off anyway, but the reason he'd kept his door closed on that particular day, was because Buffy was stretched out behind him on the living room floor.

It was not long after that, perhaps even out of a bit of pique, that Darcy hooked-up with Eddie – a guy who promptly assumed both dominant and semi-live-in status. The fights started-up regular as clockwork, right from the first week, usually beginning sometime after dinner and the first few libations. Earlier on Saturdays.

The police had already been called on several occasions. Frank, himself, only interceded once when the shouting finally turned into screaming.

Eddie had Darcy on the floor when Frank had kicked in their front door. Darcy was fighting for all she was worth, while Eddie was holding her by the hair and slapping her around – her shirt was ripped open.

The screaming, however, was coming from Lila, who was standing in the hall, her hands on her ears, standing and watching, wailing at the top of her lungs.

Eddie, his blood up, stood and took a big swing at Frank's jaw.

"You know," Frank said, not-quite amused, "I was hoping you'd do something like that."

He casually slipped Eddie's punch, stepped forward and gave him an open palm-strike in the nose. The blow was not hard enough to jam his nose-bone into his brain, but it was quite sufficient to break it. Eddie's face was suddenly a mess of blood and he would be sporting two dark and shiny black-eyes for the next two-weeks.

As Eddie's hands reflexively grabbed for his face, Frank knuckled-up a fist directly into his gut, making sure to place the blow directly beneath the sternum.

There was a wholly-satisfying, semi-shrill grunt, like the whistle on a tea-kettle, and all the fight promptly went out of Eddie. He dropped to his knees, gasping.

Not quite done, Frank grabbed his arm, spinning him into a combination elbow-lock and choke-hold, twisting good and goddamn hard, making sure they both *really* hurt, bringing Eddie up to a scream, before growling disgustedly in his face, his voice gravely, low as a purring leopard, and utterly dripping with contempt.

"I *should* kill you."

Then he pushed Eddie to the floor. And when he started struggling up to his knees, Frank gave him a for-good-measure kick, straight into his unguarded balls – just as hard as he could, and *square* in the middle.

Eddie let out a scream, dropping as if from a gunshot, back to the floor, clutching his balls.

Darcy had now sat up, buttoning her shirt, staring wide-eyed.

Lila in the hall had likewise fallen silent, gaping in awe. Now she ran to her mother, who grabbed her up, and both of them started crying.

Behind them, Julia now appeared at the kicked-in front door. Standing with her, were two uniformed cops.

The scene was pretty obvious. A crying woman with a bloody face sitting in the hall, holding a crying child – a guy standing between her and another guy, who was lying beaten-up on the floor.

Both officers moved in quickly, motioning Julia aside. They both had hands on their gun-butts – not yet drawn, but Frank knew they would remain there until he was deemed not a threat.

Eddie, moaning on the floor, still holding his balls, was clearly no danger. One of the officers led Frank outside, while the other bent, tending to Eddie.

"It's superficial," Frank offered back. "I didn't do anything permanent."

He shrugged.

"Although, I should have."

The officer on Frank's arm eyed him sternly – deliberately professionally, Frank thought. His badge said 'Hamilton' – as milquetoast, Johnny-policeman a name as you could get.

"Be careful," Hamilton said. "You assaulted that man and could be brought up on charges yourself, if we believed this was a personal matter and not an ex-soldier protecting an abused neighbor woman."

Hamilton eyed Frank seriously. He was taller than Frank, and quarterback athletic.

"I don't happen to think this is the case. But you want to watch what you say."

Hamilton glanced back and lowered his voice.

"Look, I sympathize," he said. "I see this sort of bullshit all the time. We'll take him in, but unless she presses charges, he'll be right back out. And nine times out of ten, she'll take him right back again."

"And he'll beat her up again," Frank said. "Ten times out of ten. Unless someone stops him."

"Then call *us*," Hamilton said. "That's *our* job."

Frank nodded to manager Julia, who had faded back and was now joined by Eleanor and several other neighbors from up the way.

"I'm guessing, she *did* call you," Frank said. "When seconds count, cops are minutes away."

Hamilton nodded.

"True. But if you take the law into your own hands, you better be damn sure you're right, or you could be the one going to jail."

Frank hadn't answered.

"Do we understand each other?" Hamilton pressed.

With a sigh, Frank nodded.

Eddie was taken directly to jail, although he made noises about needing a hospital. Hamilton had shrugged to his partner – '*Miller*', according to his badge – and pushed Eddie into the backseat of their cruiser.

"I think our staff-nurse can deal with your nose," Hamilton said. "Besides, it'll make a better picture for your mugshot."

Eddie was also starting to complain about being cuffed, and then something about how he couldn't breathe through his broken nose, but Miller shut the door, cutting him off, leaving him cursing mutely through the window.

Frank glanced back at Darcy and Lila, as the police cruiser pulled out of the lot. He frowned, knowing Hamilton was very likely right – Darcy wouldn't press charges.

In point of fact, not even a day passed.

Eddie spent barely seven-hours in jail, and was back in the apartment literally the next night.

Frank had given Eddie a cold, dangerous glare across the parking lot, when he'd seen him picking up the morning mail.

Eddie stared back balefully, blinking out of two shining black-eyes, before retreating back to Darcy's apartment.

Frank wondered how long it would be before it once again got bad enough for someone to call the police.

It wouldn't be Frank calling, despite what Hamilton told him.

The truth was, it felt cowardly to call the cops. Chickenshit. What good was all his training, after all?

And predictably, it wasn't very long before things at The Glen blew-up once more.

Two-weeks later, and Eddie and Darcy were fighting again – and to be fair, witnesses to the verbal exchanges broadcast clearly out their open windows, suggested Darcy egged it on like a cattle-prod.

That was the night six-year-old Lila got her arm broken.

CHAPTER 3

Frank came home to find emergency vehicles and blinking lights in his parking lot.

He'd been out drinking at a local bar – a spot called the 'Red Rooster', located a few miles down the highway back towards Boulder. It was another traveler's exit, with a truck-stop and motels. The bar had live-music, and Frank was a semi-regular.

In fact, he'd been a bit *too* regular lately – the booze-nights were something he needed to keep a lid on.

Frank was not usually a guy that drank regularly so much as a binge-drinker. In part, it reflected a lifetime of military-discipline – he worked hard and played hard. He was good on weekdays and most weekends, but on vacations and holidays, he was known to tie it on.

On the other hand, given his current lifestyle, frugal enough to live off his pension, and not really *having* to work, these periodic binges – '*howling at the moon*' – could wind-up lasting *many* moons.

In recent years, that had been a bit of a wedge that had developed between his family and friends, because those hard-partying holidays were the only time he saw them anymore. And as they all got older, drunken furloughs didn't have the appeal they did ten years ago – not even for a lot of the old army buddies, who were starting to be married and settled down.

But Frank's drinking bouts were otherwise typically few and far between – and those camping trips, or the nights out on the town with the old buddies, were becoming steadily rarer. These days, even Rodney, biggest dog of them all, was usually simply living with his latest girlfriend – a marriage-simulation that turned-over every few months.

Throw in the fact that most of them lived out of state, and suddenly Frank was most often going out on his own. Be it camping, or the local bars.

The bar nights specifically *weren't* binge-nights – he deliberately tried to take it easy, staying within the physical, if not legal limit to drive home, sticking to a few shots, and beers.

In terms of inebriation, he was borderline impaired when he turned off the exit down the access-road that led to The Glen and saw flashing police lights.

As he turned his old pick-up down into the lot, he saw more emergency vehicles gathered down at the bottom, across from the office, in front of his own apartment.

His parking spot was blocked by an ambulance and a police cruiser, so Frank pulled his truck into one of the guest spaces next to the main office.

Checking his breath briefly, making sure not to stagger, he opened the door and stepped out.

Now he saw Eddie sitting in the back of the cop car. He was cuffed, looking sullen.

Everyone else was gathered around the ambulance, where Lila was being loaded onto a stretcher.

The little girl had her arm wrapped in a sling and Darcy was hovering over her, tears running down both their cheeks.

Several other neighbors had gathered, watching. Eleanor, who lived next door, was standing at her porch, her dogs barking incessantly at her heel, tugging at their leashes.

Julia was talking to the police. Frank recognized Officers Hamilton and Miller.

Hamilton frowned when he saw Frank walking past.

Frank stopped. He was pretty soused but he didn't think he was weaving.

"The boyfriend beat the mother up," Officer Hamilton offered, without Frank having to ask. "Broke the little girl's arm."

Frank nodded slowly, saying nothing. He glanced at Julia, whose eyes were wide and teary.

"What can I say?" Hamilton said. "I wish you'd been home."

Frank looked over at little Lila being loaded on the ambulance, and then Darcy's beaten-up face – all of it so terribly predictable.

He spared Eddie a glare through the window of the cruiser. Eddie looked quickly away.

Frank nodded to Hamilton, as he turned back towards his apartment.

"Well," he said, "maybe next time."

'*Next time*' would be when Lila went missing.

CHAPTER 4

Lila disappeared on a Saturday; Frank was camping and pretty much missed it.

He'd gone off on what started as a weekend trip with several other guys – Rodney, the Jones brothers, and few others – a heavy drinking binge-weekend with enough fishing in-between to catch dinner. And since there was a general store that sold liquor less than an hour's drive from where they set camp, that first weekend extended to a week, and then ten days later, they were still out there.

The turn-out had been good this trip – Rodney was between house-mates, both Jones brothers were divorced, and even a few of the non-regulars had been given permission from their spouses.

The oldest was Bob, who'd also been married the longest, going on ten-years, and he assured Frank that even in the best marriages, there was a point where a little absence made the heart grow fonder.

Besides, they were all getting older. Frank was actually the baby of the group, at not-yet thirty-seven. And that was damn-near forty – which Bob, with his receding hair and belly-paunch, also assured them felt every bit as old as he thought it would.

This trip might be the last hurrah for most of them to be together. At least as a group. So they stretched it out a bit.

Frank actually had no particular reason to come home. He wasn't working, his pension paid the bills, and all of it was on auto-pay.

He *did* need to feed Buffy, but she really only needed to eat a couple times a month. He tended to feed her every five or six days – usually something small, like a rabbit. Snakes actually didn't normally gorge themselves, because a big lump in the belly made them cumbersome and vulnerable. In fact, constrictors were known to puke-up large meals when threatened – a stressful metabolic waste for the snake.

The rest of Buffy's care was all automatic. Her cage constantly pumped clean, fresh water, as well as sporting a sunlamp.

She was probably hungry, but pythons could go months or even years without eating, so she should be fine.

He was less certain about Darcy and Lila. He'd taken Officer Hamilton's advice and stayed uninvolved – even when Eddie was back less than a goddamn week after he'd broken that little girl's arm.

Frank saw the accelerating pattern of abuse. And frustratingly, Darcy herself was as much to blame. It wasn't like Eddie kicked the door down. Darcy got beat-up but let him back in anyway. And Frank knew she would. The bitter, angry part of himself that he hated, couldn't help but think the dumb bitch deserved it.

Eddie had avoided eye-contact with Frank in the parking lot, and currently seemed to be on his best behavior.

Darcy hadn't pressed charges on the grounds that Lila's injury had technically been an accident. Eddie hadn't been *trying* to hit the kid – she just took a good one trying to stop the assault on her mother.

Those things happened.

Darcy had seen Frank across the lot the same day

Eddie came back, and Frank frowned back at her just as sternly.

Now she wouldn't meet his eye either.

So Frank was doing his best to wash his hands of the whole thing, retreating into the sort of affected, cynical apathy he'd developed, walking past the wreckage he and his troops left behind in the villages they'd shot up overseas.

There was always the collateral. You just couldn't let yourself care too much.

Darcy was certainly not the first woman to let a sonofabitch back in.

Of course, Frank's *own* wife wasn't one of those. Barb had been calling again, leaving a string of unanswered messages on his phone.

Frank hadn't signed the divorce papers yet.

He couldn't quite achieve apathy on *that* front.

And as was his way, over the last few months, he had retreated from it all, out into the woods, always with several half-gallons of high-octanes, and as many of the old buddies he could get coaxed out with him – several of *them* being freshly-divorced veterans who came back home to wives and relationships that had dissolved while they were overseas. It was the one thing they didn't train you for.

This last trip had sort of been a binge for everybody. And none of them had any particular reason to go home.

So a long weekend ended up being two-weeks.

When his friends finally dropped Frank off, it was Sunday morning, and once again there were police lights flashing in his driveway.

CHAPTER 5

Barb had actually been over at Frank's complex earlier the same Saturday that little girl went missing. It wasn't until she got home and turned on the news, that she realized she was nearly a witness.

The afternoon anchor-girl was on – a pretty young piece of eye-candy, calling herself 'Alissa Willis', who read the report with breathless drama, as if trying out for the lead in the school play – a missing child.

Then she read the name of the complex.

Barb couldn't believe it. She'd probably missed the first ambulances by not much more than an hour.

She had gone over there looking for Frank, bound and determined to get his by-God signature, once and for all. He hadn't been answering his phone, returning messages – from her *or* her lawyers.

There were people who were stubborn, and then there was Frank Walker. He'd been fighting this divorce like a military strategist – disrupting the opponent, simply not allowing the machinery to advance. He made it look like he was just being a slacker, but Barb knew better.

This time, she'd had to get his address from her lawyers just to GPS the place – almost twenty goddamn miles out of town. She was already at a low simmer when she turned her car down into the steep driveway, and spotted his pick-up in the lower lot. She parked right next to it.

Preparing herself to be either civil or pissed-off, Barb had gone to unit 12 and rang the bell.

After a few moments, she knocked.

Then she knocked louder, her temper beginning to slip.

Until today, Frank's primary strategy was to simply not *be* there to be found. But if that failed, she knew he would be perfectly content to just sit on the couch, watching television, while she banged on the door outside.

And so Barb started banging on the door.

Then, her temper boiling over, she started kicking it too.

"*Frank!*" she shouted angrily. "You *chickenshit!* I can see your truck! I know you're in there!"

"Actually," a voice said behind her, "I don't think he is."

Barb turned to find a young woman standing behind her – twenty-something and pretty, dressed to attract, with high-cut shorts and t-shirt. She actually reminded Barb of herself just a few short years ago.

"I'm Julia," the young woman said, "I'm the manager here. I haven't seen Mr. Walker in almost two weeks. I think he's out of town."

"Where?" Barb asked.

"He didn't say. I know he camps a lot."

Barb smiled cynically.

"He goes out drinking in the woods a lot," she corrected.

Julia shrugged noncommittally.

"If you say so. But, I'm sorry. I can't have you banging on our tenant's doors. I'm going to have to ask you to leave."

Barb's eyes narrowed. For a moment, her temper threatened. But then she recognized the look in Julia's eye and nodded understanding.

That look had been in her eye a few years ago too.

"I know," Barb said. "He's cute. But trust me, honey. He's got problems."

She stepped back, with a sigh, eying Julia earnestly.

"He's not a bad guy. I don't ever want to say that. But he gets *way* too heavy on everything."

Julia said nothing, but she nodded towards the drive, indicating the exit.

Barb smiled thinly.

"Look," she said, "you obviously know him. And you clearly *like* him. So you're not trying to hear it from he. Just tell him I came by with the divorce papers. *Again*."

Barb gave Julia's tight little twenty-something figure a quick once-over.

"For what it's worth, he *is* good in the sack." Barb smiled. "If you're determined to go there. Maybe you could help convince him it's time to move on."

Julia said nothing but her eyes narrowed coldly.

Barb shrugged.

"Just sayin'."

And with that, Barb turned to leave, climbing into her little car. Julia stared balefully after her, as the little eco-rig maneuvered back up the steep narrow drive.

Julia was still stewing over the remark an hour later.

Not that she hadn't been considering exactly that, but it was still damned rude to say so.

That was when she first heard Darcy calling after her daughter, her voice only just starting to turn frightened and shrill.

CHAPTER 6

Frank got most of the story secondhand. When Rodney dropped him off at the top of the drive, he saw the emergency lights, and already had some idea what to expect.

Sure enough, Eddie was once again in the backseat, although this time, he was shouting animatedly, his eyes wide with objection.

It was barely after ten a.m. – he must have started drinking early, even for a Sunday.

Again, Frank saw Julia, standing there in tears, taking questions from Officer Hamilton.

Darcy was huddled aside with Officer Miller, her face was streaked in tears, make-up running, her hair wild. Miller had one hand on her shoulder, as if ready to restrain her.

Eleanor hovered over the younger woman's other shoulder, her barking dogs secured in the apartment today, their doggie-door locked. Several other tenants milled behind her, watching somberly – all four couples, and one of the working-Joes.

Julia turned to Frank as he came walking up.

"Lila's gone," she said, breaking into fresh tears. "Little Lila..."

Hamilton's eyes cut to Frank. There was not quite shame in them, but Frank could see self-judgment.

"The young girl disappeared yesterday," Hamilton explained, speaking in careful cop-monotone. "Last the mother knew, she was in her room playing."

According to Darcy's statement, Eddie was the one who first reported her missing. He had actually been demonstrating deliberate attentiveness, as the little girl had hobbled around the little two-bedroom apartment with a cast and a sling.

The full arm-cast had just come off, replaced by a partial brace covering her lower arm, wrapped in gauze, although she still wore the sling. She'd not been allowed to play outside since the accident – and Darcy still wasn't giving permission, but Lila had apparently stolen out into the lower grounds anyway.

Eddie, who had been in the living-room playing video-games, suddenly realized it had been over an hour since he'd seen her. Darcy, occupied in the kitchen, hadn't looked for her since declining Lila's last request to play outside.

Darcy found her daughter's sling over by the pond.

Suddenly panicked, she had immediately called the police and the fire department, and they had spent the afternoon dredging the small pond, ultimately finding nothing.

Officer Hamilton had severely questioned Eddie.

"Let's be clear, *you* were the last to see her?"

Eddie had been adamant.

"No. I was just the first to notice she was gone."

Hamilton had nodded.

"A convenient difference," he said.

The search of the surrounding area turned up nothing, but that left-behind sling was suggestive of an abduction. A public missing-child alert was sent out.

Eddie remained a free-man that night. Despite having recently caused the little girl's injury, there was nothing to indicate he'd gone anywhere. If he'd made off with Lila, it couldn't have been far, but she was nowhere to be found.

As Julia reported to Frank later, Hamilton was still looking at him closely.

"We don't know exactly what happened to that little girl yet," he told her, "so we don't know if that gives him an alibi or not."

The implication clearly being, they just didn't know *how* he did it yet.

Darcy was clearly having thoughts of her own.

After the panic and shock of that first evening settled into the morning, with still no sign of her daughter, Darcy now centered her attention on Eddie – not the last to see her, but the one who reported her missing, *and* who had broken her arm bare weeks before.

That conversation had gone badly – and loudly.

This time, Darcy started hitting him first. According to Eleanor, who was standing outside with her dogs, watching the whole thing through their open front window, Eddie was actually being restrained, and didn't start hitting her back until she'd bloodied his nose and lip.

Julia once again called the police, but as it turned out, they were already on their way. Hamilton had gotten a warrant for Eddie's arrest, intending to bring him in for more stringent questioning now that twenty-four-hours had passed and the little girl was officially a missing person.

The cops beat Frank home by about fifteen minutes. Eddie had apparently resisted, allowing Hamilton and Miller the opportunity to rough him up a little, face-planting him on the driveway, and wrenching his arms back into the cuffs.

"He was hollering that he didn't do anything," Julia told Frank later. "He was fighting them all the way."

Eddie now sat in the back of the cruiser. His shouting had subsided, but he was rocking in his seat like a test monkey in a cage.

Julia joined Eleanor at Darcy's shoulder, holding her comfortingly as Officer Miller stood, pocketing his notepad.

"We'll be in touch, ma'am," Miller said. "We'll let you know the moment we know anything new."

In the back of the cruiser, Eddie scowled.

As Hamilton opened the driver's door, he caught Frank's eye as he stood watching from the edge of the lot.

Frank eyed him back, a frown etched on his face, letting the judgment sell itself.

Hamilton said nothing as he climbed into the cruiser. The lights flashed as the cruiser pulled away, heading up the drive and out of the lot.

The other tenants had started to filter back to their own apartments. Eleanor and Julia both still sat with Darcy, whose own steady weeping seemed to have finally lapsed into an exhausted half-daze.

More collateral, Frank thought. *Too* predictable.

With affected apathy, he turned away from it all, back to his own apartment. He twisted the key in the lock, pushing open the door, blinking as his eyes adjusted to the dim light. The sunlamp on Buffy's cage was shining through the open bedroom door.

Frank froze as he saw the lid on Buffy's tank was flipped open.

He felt a grateful second of pure, sublime relief when he saw Buffy still inside.

That moment was followed by cold dawning horror when he saw the child-sized lump in her belly.

CHAPTER 7

It had been a long time, but Buffy *had* gotten out before. Besides the attack on Barb, where she had simply escaped her cage, there was twice that Buffy actually got outside.

Both were incidents Frank was very self-reproachful about. But at the same time, he was a bit prideful, in his dutiful military manner, that he had compensated and corrected.

Stories involving escaped pet pythons were common, and these cases were almost always due to irresponsibility – something Frank frowned on and was shamed to find in himself.

In his defense, both incidents happened during binge-periods when he'd been drinking *way* too much.

Didn't say it was a *good* defense.

Because responsibilities sometimes got missed.

A large constrictor loose and hungry was no joke. Pet pythons had killed children in neighboring bedrooms – again, usually a case of neglect or insufficient containment. The latter was the case the first time Buffy escaped.

It had been seven years ago, and Frank was living in a rented house in Boulder. Buffy was three years old and already nearly fifteen-feet long. She'd been secured in a locked cage, but had escaped anyway. Frank had underestimated the dramatically increased strength that came with her size, and she had simply broken out.

He had only been gone for the evening, but came home to find her lounging on his living room floor. He only knew she'd actually been out of the house because of the smallish lump in her belly – a lump that turned out to be the old lady's cat from next door.

Neighbors would later recollect Frank often helping this old woman with her groceries during the time he lived there – sometimes even buying them for her.

They talked about how modest Frank was, because he always brushed-off accolades whenever someone commented on it. The truth, of course, was that it pained him to appear altruistic when he was really only trying to allay his own guilty conscience.

He also figured the poor woman was better off thinking her cat was a runaway, or even hit by a car. '*Eaten by a snake*' didn't allow for the same warm memories. For her part, that little old lady thought Frank was just about the greatest person ever – sorry about your cat.

About a year later, Buffy had gotten out again, when Frank had briefly lived in Denver.

That time, he'd just simply left the latch to her cage unlocked.

Retrospectively, that was the one he was most ashamed of – the instance probably most attributable to his drinking. It was also the reason he'd left Denver.

He'd been gone a week that time, on an extended ski-weekend with a pair of co-eds, and a few of their sorority sisters.

Definitely a fun weekend, and they'd already been indulging in some high-octanes before they headed up to the mountains. Frank had actually been taking it easy, having been given driving chores, chauffeuring the lot of them in his truck. But he *had* taken a few tugs off the bottle before he left.

The last thing he'd done was feed Buffy and check her cage – a live rabbit – always given to her through a smaller side hatch on her cage. Frank never fed her through the main opening – that was where he did maintenance, or took her out of the cage, if she needed care or a little breathing room. The side-door was the food-trough.

This was the opening Frank had left open. Or not quite open, but unlatched.

Buffy always seemed to know when locks weren't secured. Frank had observed that, even as a small hatchling, she wouldn't poke at a locked cage – but she *would* poke an unlocked lid right open.

She had nosed that unlatched door open. It was just wide enough to accommodate her now sixteen-foot mass, and she had likewise nosed open a cracked bedroom window.

Frank was never certain what the small lump he found in her that time actually was. It could have just been a possum or a raccoon – although it *was* roughly the size of the 'missing dog' on the signs stapled to fence-posts all over the neighborhood.

On this occasion, Frank made no effort to track down the owner, but simply canceled his lease, left the property and Denver altogether. The place was shameful to him now.

The truth was, he actually considered both incidents lucky – not the least of which, because, in both cases, Buffy had made her way back *in*.

Still, Frank was personally chagrined that he'd allowed it to happen at all.

Part of it was budget – living on his pension, cutting corners. But going forward, that could no longer be allowed. Two deals like this in the service would have earned him a bust in rank. Three would be considered enemy action.

He simply needed to be more careful. You had to treat an animal like Buffy the same as owning a gun.

Frank was not a romantic about Buffy's nature – he understood perfectly well that she was a predator. And while he might love her like a pet, she did not *return* his affection. And if her instincts were activated, she would constrict and kill him as readily as any of her rabbits.

She had, in fact, wrapped on him once. She'd been seven-feet long at the time, and was starting to be a little more dominant than she had been as a hatchling.

It hadn't been a big deal – she'd constricted around his lower leg like a fifty-pound blood-pressure cuff. Frank had lump-footed his way over to the bathroom, with Buffy hanging on his leg, and plopped her under the faucet, turning hot water on her coils.

Buffy had immediately dropped away, slithering out of the path of the scalding water.

There were a number of ways to get a constrictor to let-go its hold. Very cold water would have worked too. Likewise, pouring alcohol into its mouth would also cause a python to release, as would grabbing its tail and bending the tip, although this last one was damaging to the snake.

It was always best to get them to drop their grip voluntarily, because it was damn near impossible to pull them off forcefully. Once a snake had a good solid wrap, good luck peeling the thing away, short of killing it.

People had literally cut python's heads off trying to get them to release. And prying open their jaws was like dragging your skin through a roll of barbed-wire and fish-hooks – and that was assuming you could reach the head through the mounded coils.

The fact was, constrictors could kill you quicker than any venomous snake – squeezing tight enough to freeze your circulation and stop your heart – lack of oxygen to the brain caused death in seven minutes, versus a half-an-hour for the fastest-acting venoms.

And as Frank now regarded Buffy, lounging in her cage, with the tell-tale bulge in her middle, he knew that little girl... Lila... would have been taken in seconds.

A python's strike was faster than the eye-blink reflex of a human. The first two coils would be wrapped in under a second – Lila would have been buried in coils in bare moments. She probably wouldn't even had a chance for more than a brief chirp of a scream before her breath was forced out of her.

Buffy would have held the little girl in her coils for the ritualized ten minutes, just to make sure.

Frank shut his eyes – helpless not to visualize the rest of it.

Lila was bigger than a rabbit, but she was still just a little girl – she would not have taken long to swallow.

Buffy would have retreated quickly afterwards. The weather was cloudy and overcast that day, and a cold-blooded reptile would be looking for warmth. She would also be feeling vulnerable with a large, post-feeding lump in her abdomen, and anxious to get out of sight.

And so she went back to the apartment. She would have been resting comfortably in her cage before the mother of the girl in her belly even thought to miss her.

CHAPTER 8

Frank abruptly realized he'd been standing there for nearly five minutes, staring at the snake in the cage, his bags still in hand. Belatedly, he looked back to see if he had closed the front door behind him.

As if on autopilot, his legs stiff as a robot, he walked over to Buffy's tank and pulled the lid shut.

Vacantly, blankly, he snapped the latch, testing it quickly as he did so.

There was nothing wrong with it.

He must have left it open the last time he'd fed her. It had been the day he left. He hadn't even been drinking yet. Rodney was supposed to pick him up in an hour, and Frank had been giving Buffy's cage a quick once-over. He'd fed her through her trough – another live rabbit – and then spruced-up her cage while she spent her typical ten minutes constricting and swallowing.

When Rodney had picked him up and handed him an open bottle across the seat, that was his first drink of the day. He'd been cold sober.

That meant, he'd just absentmindedly left the latch unlocked.

As easily as that. He didn't even have the excuse of being drunk yet.

Frank's head pulsed at the temple. He wondered if he might actually be having a stroke. In about sixty-seconds he was already pacing rapidly through the stages of shock, horror, and denial – but he was getting hung-up on the acceptance. He could literally *feel* his mind stuttering on that part like a scratch on a CD.

Frank realized he was shaking his head slowly, back-and-forth, like an animatronic construct stuck on the same repetitive motion.

Every part of his conscious and subconscious mind was rejecting the input of his eyes – blocking all the images forming involuntarily in his mind.

He couldn't fucking *live* with this.

The thought of even looking at himself in a mirror...?

Or the thought of having other people SEE? To KNOW?

He might actually have to kill himself.

Frank looked down at Buffy, and for a moment, his face cracked – a soldier – a veteran who had seen violent death as well as caused it – and for an instant, he broke, as if to weep like a despairing child.

But before the first tear dropped, the stone fell, and his face went emotionless and slack.

Perhaps it *was* a small stroke. Or maybe he was in some sort of shock.

Either way, now he was calm. And he began to function again, looking down at the situation in front of him.

This was not his war-face. This was a system on reboot, proceeding one operation at a time.

He took a breath, and looked down at Buffy with grim resolution.

First thing was first. She had to go. And this time, she had to be put down.

Frank would mourn her, because none of it was her fault. The blame was all his.

And when he ended her life, that would be his fault

too.

But... he would have to wait.

He couldn't put her down now, or even give her away, because she still had her last meal inside her – and would for the next six-to-ten days.

Frank had to wait for any trace evidence to digest.

Then there would be nothing left.

And people would never know.

Then he could start worrying about the mirror.

But even as he thought it, he caught his reflection in the window – a ghost image.

He saw the fear in his own eyes – and that was definitely different from his war-face. So was the self-loathing. The dark circles weren't from this morning's hangover.

Yep. That mirror was definitely going to be a problem.

Frank turned away. He had to at least get through the next week to ten days. That meant he had to live with it until then.

That also meant without any booze-Novocain. It was time to put that aside for real.

He shut his eyes, already imagining the next several days.

Lord, he wanted a drink.

That night, he went to sleep with his service pistol in his hand. The hammer was cocked, the safety off, and the barrel was to his head.

This... *feeling* inside him – he could make it stop, whenever he wanted to.

But eventually, he fell asleep. He did not dream.

He woke up the next morning with his finger still on the trigger, the gun lying on the pillow, still aimed lazily at his temple.

There was knocking at the door.

CHAPTER 9

Officer Hamilton was back at The Glen, interviewing neighbors. The boyfriend – Eddie – was sticking to his story pretty doggedly, and Hamilton was making sure there wasn't any doubt.

As a cop, he very much wanted to nail the son of a bitch to the wall.

Knowing that, as an investigator, he also understood that he had to be careful about seeing what he wanted to see.

Eddie was a real case-file, for sure. He was openly admitting to beating-up his girlfriend and her kid, both. And *that* was supposed to be his alibi.

Hamilton had seen logic like that at play in perps before – If I confess to *this*, I surely wouldn't have a problem confessing to *that* – so obviously I didn't do it.

At the surface, it was the sort of thing a kid would say. A parent's appropriate response would be: *this* time you got *caught*.

But Eddie wasn't confessing. He was holding to his guns – loudly, in fact.

And... pretty convincingly.

As a cop, Hamilton's eyes had always been set on being a detective. He didn't like vice – that was where you saw all the day-to-day bullshit.

Hamilton wanted to solve cases. Part of that was learning to read people.

Eddie was a dirt-bag. Hamilton knew it, and didn't

like him. He considered Eddie the obvious suspect.

That was his opinion going-in.

But attempting to look at him for the first time, Hamilton might have actually believed him about this.

The fact was, Eddie wasn't showing the tells of a liar, which were mostly mannerisms betraying the fear reflex of being caught.

Fear was there, but his overall posture was more like the self-righteous anger of the unjustly accused. The fear Hamilton saw was the sort of thing he'd seen when the suspect knew it still *looked* bad.

Hence, the confessional-reasoning stage – it was clearing the air.

Hamilton still believed he had his man. At this point, he thought he just had a good, self-motivated liar. But because it was his job, and because he *wanted* to bury this guy, he would make sure to eliminate all other possibilities first.

That military guy – Walker – would probably be a good person to talk to. He would be trained to keep an eye out for oddities – any prowler creeping about, eyeballing kids. The place was off the highway, after all, and there were sometimes drifters hitching along the road.

Eleanor, the old lady, was another one Hamilton wanted to speak with. He recognized her as the sort prone to watch out windows, sometimes with binoculars. She was also the Chapman woman's next-door neighbor.

Then there was that pretty desk girl, Julia. As Miller, his partner, had commented, she might be worth interviewing just for the sake of her legs alone.

Hamilton had shaken his head warily. He was always extra-professional when he was questioning a particularly good-looking woman – sexual harassment suits were filed these days over facial-twitches and eye-blinks.

Julia's office was right across from the missing girl's apartment, and she would have had a constant view from her desk. She had in fact, seen the little girl out playing – the first time since she'd had her cast on.

But she also spent a lot of time looking at her computer screen or down at her phone.

Still, Hamilton would have thought a strange man walking around the lot would have caught her eye. The complex was on a sharp incline – it was a bit of a chore just to walk, and not a place a car could get in and out of quickly – and again, a vehicle would be noticed.

These were, of course, a number of questions that remained, even if Eddie remained the chief suspect. The truth was, they still didn't know exactly what happened to that little girl.

Her loose sling left behind was an indication that she had been grabbed, but where had she been spirited off to? And how? Perhaps a car waiting up on the main access-road? If so, how had Eddie, operating on his own, gotten her out of there? They'd searched the pond and the surrounding woods, and gotten nothing. And as far as they knew, Eddie hadn't gone anywhere.

That was a significant hole for the prosecution, and one Hamilton knew he had to plug if he wanted Eddie convicted.

Hamilton turned his cruiser into the lot, making his way down to the main office. He decided to go to the soldier's place first.

When he knocked, it was a minute before Frank answered. Then the door opened just a crack.

Frank stared out, not appearing pleased over the

morning disturbance. His eyes looked sunken and Hamilton wondered if he might be hungover, although he didn't smell like alcohol.

He kept the door mostly shut, blocking the view into the apartment.

"Officer... Hamilton, was it? Can I help you?"

Frank's tone was not particularly inviting. Hamilton wondered if he held the police responsible for that little girl. After intervening on the mother's behalf that night, the law had, after all, practically threatened him away.

"Well," Hamilton said, "I know you weren't here, but I could still use your statement concerning Mr. Quist's past behavior."

"Haven't you already got all that?" Frank said, eyeing Hamilton meaningfully. "From the last time?"

"We're trying to be thorough," Hamilton said. "This time there will be charges, and probably a prosecution, so we need to make the case stick."

"I'm sorry," Frank said, "but I'm a little under the weather."

Hamilton nodded.

"It doesn't have to be today. But if you could call the station, in the next few days, we'd like to get a more detailed statement."

Frank sighed.

"Fine," he said, and started to pull back inside.

"You know," Hamilton said, "I was giving you the official line when I told you not to take the law into your own hands." He shook his head. "But this is the second time I'm saying I wish you'd been here."

Frank's expression was grim.

"No doubt," he said. "I wish I'd been here too."

He shook his head.

"You have no idea how much I wish I'd been

here."

Frank stepped back into his apartment and pulled the door firmly shut behind him.

CHAPTER 10

When Barb called later that morning, Frank surprised her and answered.

He supposed his defenses were down. For the last several weeks, he'd been avoiding her to the best of his ability. But that had actually been his strategy for keeping her.

Now?

Well, that was pretty much over, wasn't it? What would she say, what would she think, if she *knew*?

Up to now, he believed she still thought well of him, even if she didn't want to *be* with him.

Frank absolutely could not take how she would look at him if it all came out – especially considering the snakebite scars on her own leg.

So perhaps part of the reason he answered the phone was to run a little intercept for any ideas that might creep into that active little mind of hers.

He also conceded that maybe – just maybe – the small weak part of himself needed to hear her voice.

It didn't help. Barb was combative right from the start.

"I don't believe it," she said. "*The* Frank Walker. I've only been trying to reach you for the last three months."

"Well," Frank replied, affecting his standard witticism, "You're not the first woman to come chasing me down."

"I sent you the papers again."

Frank tisked, because that's what she would expect.

"Haven't seen them."

"Have you looked?"

"Nope. No reason to check the mail, really. All the bills are paid automatically. The junk-mail tends to pile up."

"I've sent emails, texts," Barb said, her voice starting to rise. But then she stopped, taking a controlling breath.

"Frank," she said, "this is eventually going to get done with your cooperation or not. You're just making this all harder."

Frank allowed this was so.

"It's not supposed to be easy," he replied. "You're the one that left. I kept my vows."

That jerked her temper off its leash.

"Maybe you forgot about the one that said *'protect'*."

Frank shut his eyes, already knowing where she was going.

"I saw that little kid missing on the news," she said hotly. "Your damned snake didn't *eat* her, did it?"

Frank knew Barb was angry. She didn't really *think* that – it was just a mean, angry thing to say.

Still, it *had* obviously crossed her mind, so his response had to be correct.

"Very funny," he said, his tone dismissive, with just the right touch of irritation, letting her know she'd touched the button she'd wanted to push – which also gave him the cover to move past it, leaving the remark quickly forgotten.

"They arrested the boyfriend," Frank said, offering up a little deflection.

"I saw that too. The news said there had been other incidents in recent weeks and that on at least one occasion, neighbors were *'forced to intercede, leading to blows'*.'"

Barb snickered a little.

"I think they added that part to make sure the police didn't get blamed when they posted the guy's mugshot. A big busted nose and two black-eyes."

She sighed.

"Now, who do I know living there who might account for that guy's face?"

"No comment," Frank said.

"I thought so," Barb said, with another deep resigned sigh. "Frank, you are incurably a good guy."

There was an excruciating pause while Frank absorbed this misconception, hating himself for it, but not contradicting it.

"You're a good guy," Barb repeated. "Now will you sign the papers? Will you just please let me go?"

Frank felt the dart in his heart.

He knew she deserved to be free. And she was about to get her wish.

Just not yet.

Frank glanced back at Buffy in her cage – the lump in her belly was already significantly distended just since yesterday.

Lila hadn't been very big. She would be gone soon enough.

But in the meantime, he still had to wait. That meant keeping up appearances.

"Let me go, Frank," Barb asked again.

"You already left," Frank said, and hung-up.

He sat there for several minutes, waiting to see if she would call back.

In the background, the TV was on, showing the news. Frank had been watching the coverage on Eddie – they showed the mugshot with his two shiners.

The reporter on-screen was really playing up the domestic-abuse angle. On top of the little girl's disappearance, it was the perfect sordid little press-case.

They dug up other cases of abuse in Eddie's background before Darcy. Frank was not surprised to learn he'd been arrested before. And none of the other women had ever pursued charges either.

Without the fact of the missing little girl, he would have moved on to somebody else – probably continuing on the same way for his whole life.

Frank had no doubt that was true – which made all the rest of it easier to rationalize.

Accountability was at the heart of justice.

Of course, this time, Frank held himself most accountable of all.

He had wanted to act on that accountability that first day – he'd slept with his service pistol at his head for those first few nights. It was a special punishment that he had to wait.

For the next several days, Frank sat there in his apartment, watching the coverage of his crime on television, doing his best not to check too often on Buffy's cage.

He stayed away from the booze, although the pangs were strong – as was the proactive urge to simply *do* something, when all that could practically be done was sit and wait.

A special punishment – he knew he deserved it.

But after that first week, when the bulge in Buffy's belly was mostly gone, the urgency started to fade.

CHAPTER 11

It was now two weeks since Lila Chambers disappeared.

The lump in Buffy's gut had been gone for several days.

It was time, Frank thought, to finally get down to it. He'd been procrastinating.

After the third night, he'd stopped sleeping with his pistol. He hoped he wasn't learning to live with it.

But he knew if he waited long enough, he would. The wars overseas had taught him that much. There were things that he would suddenly stop-short out of nowhere and remember – but he didn't dwell on them – they didn't keep him up at nights.

Not anymore, at least.

But Frank didn't want to let this go cold.

The plan this weekend was to take Buffy out into the woods, deep up into the mountains, and dispose of her there. A quick bullet to the brain. He could burn the carcass in his campfire.

Then there would be nothing left.

He could decide the next step once that part was done.

His beard had grown out over the last two weeks – that damned shaving mirror kept looking back at him.

Frank was already packed, and ready to start loading his gear into his truck. Last step would be to load Buffy into her crate. With her weighing over three-hundred pounds, it was a bit of a heave-and-grunt getting her off the hand-truck into his truck-bed, especially when she was just coiled-up as dead-weight in a container. But he couldn't exactly ask anyone for help.

He also needed to do it quickly and discreetly – neighbors notice people throwing around heavy loads.

His truck was already parked directly opposite the view from Julia's office window, so that anything he loaded into the back would be out of her sight.

The military-strategist translated well to covering-up criminal action.

He was about to pull out Buffy's crate and start getting her ready for the trip – her *last* trip – when he was startled by a sudden loud and urgent banging at his front door.

For a moment, Frank wondered if Officer Hamilton was back, but then he heard Eleanor.

"Mr. Walker!" she gushed frantically, as Frank opened the door. "He's back! They're fighting again! It's bad!"

Frank's eyes turned across the lot.

It was barely mid-morning, not even eleven – but the front door was wide open. He saw Julia standing just outside, poised as if to run herself, her phone at her ear – no doubt once again calling the police.

Frank heard shouting from the apartment. He recognized Darcy's voice, screaming hysterically, nearly unintelligibly, "Don't you *touch* me, you *bastard!"*

Then he heard Eddie.

"*Bitch!* I didn't DO it!"

Then Frank heard a gunshot.

Julia screamed.

Frank pushed past Eleanor and was sprinting across the lot. He pulled Julia quickly back from the open door, before risking a quick look inside.

Darcy was on the ground. Her face was bloody, but Frank didn't think it was hers – it looked like splatter from Eddie's brains, which she'd just blown-out all over the wall.

Eddie was currently twitching on the floor beside her.

Darcy turned the gun on Frank as he stepped into the room. Her eyes were wide and her hands shaking, but there didn't seem to be anything wrong with her aim. It looked like she'd pelted Eddie dead between the eyes.

Frank held his hands up.

"Easy," he said. "It's all over. You're safe now."

She kept the gun aimed unerringly as Frank slowly stepped towards her, and finally kneeled down beside her. Instead of reaching for the gun still in his face, he touched a gentle hand on her shoulder.

"It's going to be okay, now," he said.

Darcy burst into tears, dropping the gun and letting it rattle onto the floor. It spun into a puddle of Eddie's blood.

Now she grabbed Frank, clinging to him with a drowner's-grip, and bawled into his arms.

He held her, remembering the night he moved in – how she came over, tarted-up, with that look in her eye, and Frank had sent her away – because Buffy had been lying on the floor behind him.

What would she say if she knew what really happened to her daughter? Would she be clinging to him so tightly?

But she didn't know. So Frank held her.

Julia stood behind them at the door, looking in, her phone at her ear, crying herself.

Frank held Darcy, letting her weep, and waited for the sounds of sirens.

CHAPTER 12

According to Officer Hamilton, Eddie had made a run for it.

The police arrived at The Glen in force this time – five cars and ten officers – this little complex had been a lot more trouble than its weight in recent days.

And mostly for purposes of clean-up, they also brought an ambulance.

Frank had turned the sobbing Darcy over to a female trauma-officer, who shunted her quickly off aside, sequestering her in the back of her cruiser.

Hamilton regarded Eddie's sprawled corpse where it lay, being documented and photographed.

Shaking his head, he turned to Frank and Julia – witnesses, waiting their turn. Julia had taken the opportunity to grab the comfort spot Darcy just vacated under Frank's arm. She was still sobbing herself, and kept her eyes deliberately averted from Eddie on the floor. Frank tolerated the contact, his own face grim and unreadable.

"Not to speak ill of the dead," Hamilton said, "but they were about to let the sonofabitch go."

Julia blanched.

"They *were*? After what happened to that little girl?"

Hamilton shook his head.

"They don't know *what* happened to that girl. And it turns out Eddie was playing on-line video games during most of the time-frame in which she disappeared."

Hamilton frowned.

"I told the DA's office there's too much uncertainty about the time for that to clear him. They told me, *that* meant they didn't have enough to hold him."

Now he coughed a bitter laugh.

"The idiot was literally being transferred out of holding to be released when he got away."

"How did he escape?" Julia asked.

Hamilton sighed.

"He was being walked out the yard to the bus and he just made a run for it. The cop that was escorting him was too damned fat and overweight to catch him.

"Not," Hamilton allowed, "that it likely would have mattered anyway."

He glanced from Eddie's corpse to where the trauma-officer was consoling Darcy.

"He was already under a restraining order," Hamilton said. "He wasn't supposed to be anywhere near her or this apartment. But that was the first damn thing he did. If he'd stuck around long enough for us to let him out, it just would have taken him another couple hours to get here."

Eleanor, sharing her wall with Darcy, filled in most of the gaps as to what happened after Eddie arrived – the ensuing conversation next-door was at full-volume and not hard to follow.

Eddie showed-up, still in jail-pants and a stolen jacket he'd taken off the bus. He confronted Darcy with the same adamant denial he'd given the police. And like the police, Darcy had been skeptical.

In days past, Darcy always submitted to Eddie's temper, but that was before she'd lost her daughter.

This time, when Eddie reached for her, "Don't you *touch* me!" was backed-up by a gunshot as she planted a bullet dead in the center of his forehead.

Darcy, even now, still had bits of Eddie's brains speckled in her face and hair.

"That means he was right on top of her," Hamilton said. "That supports her story."

"Are you going to arrest her?" Frank asked.

Hamilton shook his head.

"No. We're questioning her. She's already got history with this guy. He escaped jail and broke a restraining-order. But we do need to get the whole story, so we can clear her." He shook his head resolutely. "I don't want any of this to blow back on her."

Hamilton eyed them both frankly.

"Part of me wants to say it's for the best, but I'm not quite that cynical yet. This is just a total shit-situation."

Frank said nothing. Hamilton eyed him, perhaps wondering if he was being judged or blamed. Then he turned his attention to Eleanor, who had patiently been waiting her turn.

Julia became aware she was still clinging to Frank. Suddenly self-conscious, she disengaged, looking up at him shyly, her eyes only now drying of tears.

A pretty young thing, Frank thought wistfully, and as she looked up at him, the opportunity for simple human comfort seemed so attractive, and even possible.

For just a second, he fantasized that he could start over – forget Barb, and just move-on. Julia would be as good a place to start as any.

But Frank had a dark little secret.

How much would she like him if she *knew*?

He *wasn't* one of the good guys – not anymore.

Julia caught the look in his eye – a sad moment of

longing – and Frank blinked quickly away, lest she take it as encouragement.

"Listen," Frank announced abruptly, addressing Hamilton and the other officers, but glancing briefly at Julia, "I've got a road-trip planned this weekend. And I've got some packing to do. Are you done with me?"

Hamilton glanced at Miller and the other officers, then nodded affirmatively to Frank.

Frank nodded to Julia, still speaking to Hamilton, as he turned back to his place.

"I'll be gone a few days," he called back. "You've got my number."

As he headed back to his apartment, Frank felt Julia eyeing him quizzically. He knew he was giving her mixed-signals, but deliberately did not look back – he could not even go there right now.

For now, he turned to the more pressing business at hand.

His schedule had been pushed back a little. He would have to wait until the cops and emergency vehicles cleared the lot before he started loading his truck.

It would probably be best if he not start wrestling with his pet python, just yet.

The incident across the way had actually solved one of his problems, but it also created another.

Frank had been rationalizing hard, justifying sending another man to prison for his own irresponsibility.

Stories about Eddie's past were still coming out – more abuse, and more women willing to tell the tale. Frank was satisfied he was certainly the *sort* who might end up killing a kid by accident, and then hiding the body after he did it. He just didn't happen to have done it *this* time.

Basically, his rationalizing mind was attempting to convince his unwilling conscience that the man deserved prison for things he'd already done.

Of course, Frank was now absolved of any concern that Eddie would see false-imprisonment.

Unfortunately, there was still the matter of the missing little girl.

Eddie, after all, was set to be released. Hamilton was obviously skeptical, but the timing of his alibi was solid enough for a child-abduction, and possible murder suspect to be let go.

If it turned out they could definitely prove Eddie actually *didn't* do it, that not only left the mystery of who *did*, but also made Darcy's own actions at least partly misdirected, and possibly even criminal.

Eddie was using his hands on her – Darcy specifically said he'd grabbed her this time, not hitting right away, but shaking her like an angry parent, shouting for her to *listen* to him – a man who had abused both her and her missing daughter.

But if he wasn't actually a child-murderer... well, the guy was *dead*. It was not inconceivable, some lawyer somewhere might try to call that manslaughter – or even murder.

Best-case scenario, the mystery of Lila Chapman's disappearance died with Eddie Quist.

Just let him be some dirt-bag shot dead by his abused girlfriend.

Frank nodded to himself.

See how easy it was to rationalize?

As he sat alone in his apartment, he caught his face in the mirror.

There was no pity there.

He'd not quite made the final decision, yet, but

knew he still had his own accountability to face.

But there were still a few things that needed to be done first – a final settling of affairs.

Frank sat down at his desk, opened the top drawer, and pulled out the divorce papers Barb had sent him – one of *many* copies she'd sent over the previous weeks and months.

Without bothering to read the tiny print, Frank simply signed all the highlighted x-spots.

When he was finished, he brought up his wife's number on his phone and called her.

Barb's voice was surprised and doubtful – almost worried – at this unexpected, and radical departure from established protocol.

"Frank? Are you okay? I've been watching the news. I saw that woman..."

"That's not it," he interrupted. "I'm calling because..."

Frank cleared his voice, and for a moment, he teared-up ever so slightly.

"You win," he said. "I signed the papers. I'll drop them in the mail today."

There was a heartbeat of silence, as she absorbed this. When she spoke, he heard the urgency – she'd had the football yanked away before.

"I can come over and pick them up *now*...," she began, but Frank interrupted her.

"No need. They're signed. It's done. You win."

He glanced out the window. The emergency vehicles were all finally pulling out of the lot – the ambulance driving with the lights off. Darcy was sitting in the back of one of the police cruisers.

"Listen," Frank said, "I'm headed out of town for the next few days." He chuckled a little, ironically. "Bad cell-coverage area. So you may not hear from me for a while. I just..."

He shut his eyes.

"I signed those papers," Frank said, "because you deserve better than to be tied to my life any longer."

He took a breath, getting it all out.

"I want you to be happy," he said. "I really did love you."

Barb's reply was ready enough.

"I really did love you too," she said. "It was never about that. And I want you to be happy too."

"Goodbye, Barb," Frank said, and started to hang-up.

"Frank...?" Barb said quickly.

He paused, his finger on the button

"Thank you, Frank," Barb said.

Then she hung-up.

Frank looked down at her disconnected number onscreen. It was probably the last time he would ever call her.

He shut his eyes, allowing himself one last throb of heartache, before he let her go.

Then he stood, setting his shoulders purposefully. It was time for the next chore.

He turned for the bedroom.

Buffy needed to be loaded into her crate. He couldn't put it off any longer. She had to be put down.

CHAPTER 13

Frank had provisioned for three days in the woods. He really had no plan beyond that.

He was going to a spot high up to the end of the navigable old logging roads. Buffy and her crate together were pushing three-hundred-and-fifty pounds. He wasn't going to be lugging her up into the brush.

There was a spot he and some of his army buddies had gone – Rodney had christened it the '*Top of the World*.' It was an old defunct logging-site, that had been zoned out of existence, so the area was unkempt and overgrown. But it was a good level spot for a tent and a campfire.

It was his first trip up there alone – ordinarily, a pretty far-out trip to take-on solo, let alone with only three-day's supplies.

But maybe that was the point.

He'd always said his retirement plan was a simple one – when he got too old to take care of himself, he'd just head off into the woods and commune with the Great Spirit.

Maybe that was this time.

He shook his head. First thing was first. This trip was about one final little chore.

Frank began setting up Buffy's travel-box. It was specially-designed and remarkably compact, as was Buffy herself – it was always amazing how she could cram her length into small spaces.

She lay there in her tank, watching him through the glass, unsuspecting – perhaps recognizing her travel-box – maybe even anticipating a road-trip – and no doubt trusting her lifelong benefactor, even as he plotted her end.

Trust in me. Just in me.

That was Kaa's song – the python from Disney's version of the *Jungle Book.*

Kaa had actually been Frank's first childhood interest in snakes, and pythons in particular – those goggly cartoon eyes – somehow malevolent and joyful at the same time.

Happy to see you.

But not in a good way.

Except today, *he* was the one sidling up with bad intentions.

Frank knew she was just a reptile, and not capable of returning the affection he felt for her. But he still knew she recognized him, often rearing at his presence – not aggressively, but to take the scratch behind the neck like a pet dog.

Today he would be taking advantage of that trust.

At least, it should make everything relatively painless. Buffy was accustomed to regular travel, and not bothered or particularly stressed by being in her crate or the back of a truck.

Once they got up into the hills, Frank's plan was simply to let her out, maybe let her crawl around a bit, before he finally put his service pistol to her head and blew her peanut-wide brains out.

Then she would go into the campfire.

Frank opened the lid to Buffy's cage.

She was probably hoping to be fed – it had been two-weeks since she'd eaten, because Frank had wanted to make sure her last meal was completely digested.

On impulse, Frank grabbed a chicken-carcass out of the fridge. Normally, he fed Buffy her meals live, but he kept a couple whole-hens on hand. Pythons don't eat carrion, so you had to shake it a little, to create the impression of live-prey, to get the snake to strike and then coil.

It was also his habit – a more religious one – to feed Buffy through the smaller food-trough-door on the side, so as not to associate anything reaching through the *top* of the cage, like say Frank, himself, as food.

After today, however, conditioning wouldn't matter. Frank simply waved the chicken through the cage lid.

Behind him, there was a knock at the door.

Frank turned, he recognized Julia's shadow through the curtained window. He sighed. He'd seen that look in her eyes. It was his own fault. He'd given her the eyes first.

He started to turn, reaching to close the cage lid, but as his attention was diverted, Buffy came up and out of the cage, going after the chicken-carcass in his hand.

Frank grunted in pain as the python's teeth sunk into both the dead bird, but also his hand.

He felt the sudden jerk from more than three-hundred pounds of coiled steel muscle as Buffy threw her coils up and around him.

Then his breath was taken away as she wrapped.

CHAPTER 14

Julia had been closing the office up for the day, when she noticed Frank's truck still parked in front of his apartment.

He said he was going out of town. Hadn't he left yet? Or perhaps a friend had picked him up like last time.

Julia hadn't seen any other cars – unless he met them up on the street rather than navigate The Glen's narrow parking lot.

As she locked the office door, she regarded Darcy's empty apartment across the lot. Crime-scene tape was pasted across the door.

Darcy hadn't been back. Officer Hamilton said she wasn't being arrested, but she didn't seem in any shape to be left on her own. Julia knew her mother lived in downtown Boulder, and figured she must be staying there tonight.

That was the problem with being a landlord, even just at the local office-level. You were involved in people's lives by nature of your job, but ultimately, it wasn't supposed to be any of your business.

Like Frank, for instance.

She'd noticed the look he'd given her earlier. He also seemed to catch himself, as if pulling it back, but it was there.

On impulse, instead of heading up the hill to her own apartment, she veered off to Frank's front door and knocked.

She wondered briefly exactly what she was doing. Frank's ex – Barb – warned that he had issues, and while perhaps in a bit of a temper, she had struck Julia as sincere.

So what was she doing on his front step? Was it just her own bleeding heart?

Or maybe it was because of the other thing Barb had deliberately mentioned, when she assured Julia that Frank was good in the sack.

Pretty it up all you want, but that was an element. Would she be knocking on his door despite all this shit, if she didn't basically, sort-of, maybe have the hots for him?

Oh, what the hell, Julia thought, and rapped on the door again.

She waited a few moments. She thought she heard movement from inside after the first knock. But when she put her ear to the door, there was nothing.

The lights were off, and the curtains were closed.

Julia hesitated, wondering if he was in there and just blowing her off.

He *had* after all, broken the eye-contact he'd given her. That suggested a guy who didn't want to go forward, despite a physical attraction.

It also confirmed some of those issues Barb had mentioned – he had a tendency to get heavy – *way* too heavy, as she put it.

Julia waited a moment longer.

If he was home, he wasn't answering, which should be answer enough.

Maybe she should just let the poor guy be.

With a shrug, Julia turned and made her way back up the hill.

CHAPTER 15

It had been two days since Frank called, and Barb was waiting patiently. Buffy, herself, would have been proud.

The mail had come and gone twice, and Barb hadn't even bothered to check it – nor called her lawyer. Frank's signed-papers shouldn't be there for at least a couple of days.

He sounded sincere this time. Barb was cautiously optimistic.

Still, unlike Buffy, who Frank doted on, history had conditioned Barb to... *not* get what she was expecting.

That was not necessarily to say she hadn't gotten what she was promised.

And speaking of Buffy...

Barb saw on the news that the boyfriend – the one that got shot – had actually been due to be released.

Officer Hamilton had been interviewed several times – by earnest-looking anchor-woman Alissa Willis – and the police department's official statements were very carefully worded.

"The timeline of the girl's disappearance made it impossible to hold him," Hamilton told her, briefly. "And as of now, his alibi still seems to hold up."

Alissa Willis, wielding her microphone like a scepter, had pounced on the elephant that statement left standing in the room.

"If his alibi is solid, what else might have

happened to that little girl?"

"We don't know if his alibi is solid or not, because we still don't know what happened to her. We haven't found a body, so we don't even know for sure if she's alive or dead. She could have been grabbed by someone else. She might even have been snatched by a cougar or a coyote. We're just a ways down out of the mountains, after all."

Cougar or coyote, Barb noted.

Hamilton was suggesting Lila Chapman had been taken by an animal.

And helplessly, relentlessly, Barb's own thoughts turned that way as well – although, she wasn't thinking 'cougar'.

She looked down at the bite-marks on her leg.

Barb felt a momentary impulse to call the cops, just over the picture forming in her mind.

Calling the police on him sure as hell would not improve relations with the ex. If fact, it might very likely get him in trouble just for having the snake. Barb could speak to fair certainty that he was keeping the thing there without that little twit at the front-desk knowing about it. She knew it had also been illegally purchased and brought into the country in the first place.

Barb shut her eyes. She could just picture the meltdown if Frank found out she called the cops.

On the other hand, she *was* trying to end relations once and for all.

Her hand hovered briefly over her phone.

She wasn't *completely* a bitch, but Frank always said she could play one on TV.

Barb picked-up the phone and tapped the screen.

After a moment, she put it back down again.

Not completely a bitch.

Besides, she didn't *really* think Frank's python had anything to do with that missing girl. It was probably more about her own paranoia and peace of mind. Maybe there was even a little jealousy over the fact that, when push came to shove, Frank had chosen that damned snake over *her*.

Barb briefly felt the bitch-impulse rise back to the surface. She took a breath and let the moment pass.

She started checking her mail the following day, to find the signed-papers had not yet arrived.

The day after that, she called her lawyers to see if they'd received their copies.

She didn't really start getting pissed-off until a full week had gone by and there was still nothing.

Finally, frustrated, she started calling him again.

And once again, she started getting no answer, and her calls went directly to voicemail.

CHAPTER 16

Buffy was living quite comfortably. Affluently, even.

The apartment's bills were all on auto-pay, and Frank's pension was automatically deposited, keeping the water on, the filters in the cage pumping, the ambient temperature nice and tropical. Buffy's days were basically spent lounging in a hot-tub under a sunlamp.

She spent most of that first couple of weeks after she killed Frank simply digesting him. He was right at the practical size-limit for a python's prey – probably more than fifty-percent of her own body-weight.

The truth was, snakes of most species usually eschewed such big meals because it left them vulnerable and immobile, with a big bulky lump in their gut. In fact, when threatened, big constrictors were known to violently puke-up large meals, freshly-swallowed, regurgitating the extra weight, so they could either fight or escape. It was a costly bio-mechanical effort that squandered valuable calories.

But with her own apartment, Buffy had no need to roam. She just curled up under her artificial sun and slept it off.

Consuming Frank had taken about half-an-hour. Even large constrictors were known to have trouble swallowing humans, particularly adult men, because of their wider shoulders, combined with the fact that a snake's mouth doesn't spread as wide side-to-side as it does top-to-bottom.

But Buffy was over twenty-four-feet long. She also took the approach demonstrated by other large retics who had successfully swallowed humans. Pythons typically swallowed prey head-first, but rather than starting over the top with Frank lying on his back, which caused his shoulders to catch on her cheeks, she rolled him on his side, so she was able to walk the tips of her jaws over his shoulders instead.

At the same time, those crushing coils twisted his joints askew, pushing his head tight against his right shoulder.

Now that her jaws were able to stretch over the widest part of him, she began to crawl her body down.

That stage went quickly. Frank's feet were last down her gullet, shoes and all. A snake ate *everything*.

Frank weighed a hundred-and-eighty-pounds. He would have noted, perhaps with pride, that made him a world-record-sized meal ever recorded for a reticulated python. Or any snake for that matter.

But Frank was gone.

And since then, Buffy had lived leisurely. Decadently. With all the automatic comforts, and all the bills paid, she barely felt the need even to move.

Just... digest.

But after a couple of weeks, she started to get hungry again.

CHAPTER 17

Since the shooting, things around The Glen had been quiet – but it was the sort of quiet one hears in the aftermath of a loud explosion, after your ears stopped ringing.

Julia was still a bit shell-shocked, and was not happy to see Barb pulling her car up in front of Frank's apartment, right next to his pick-up.

The truck had been sitting in its same spot for more than two weeks. Julia hadn't seen Frank since she'd tried knocking on his door. She assumed one of his army friends must have picked him up. And it wasn't the first time he'd been gone this long.

Julia was guessing Barb hadn't heard from him either – she appeared to be in a mood. Julia rolled her eyes.

It had already been a morning. Eleanor had spent an hour out looking for one of her little barking dogs that had apparently gotten lost. Her raspy old-lady voice carried, echoing through the little gully – a little too reminiscent of a mother calling for her lost daughter.

The missing dog had Julia wondering if there wasn't a local coyote pack, somewhere – the coyote-ploy was literally named after the way they would lure domestic dogs into their pack, and then turn on them, killing and eating them.

That led to uneasy speculation as to what might

have happened to little Lila. Officer Hamilton had mentioned the possibility of an animal, during his interview.

Julia shuddered at the possibility of that little girl being dragged off into the woods, her body left exposed to the elements, no doubt gnawed-on, and then left to decompose, like so much carrion road-kill.

What could possibly be worse than that?

Of course, if that were the case, you'd think the search dogs would have turned up something.

Eleanor had eventually given up, going back inside. The old lady was visibly upset, and Julia was just thinking about checking on her, when she saw Barb driving up.

Julia, who was pursuing a degree in social-work and counseling, and specifically striving to learn how to be most patient with people, muttered a litany of curses. She did not need this shit today.

Barb climbed out of her car, stopping briefly to look at Frank's truck. Barb frowned, rubbing at the small layer of dust that had gathered on the windshield.

Then she turned to his front-step and rapped smartly on the door.

"Frank? If you're there, please open up. I want to talk."

She rapped again. When there was no response, she peered in the curtained windows.

Then she turned, looking for the office, and spotted Julia through the window. Barb waved, beckoning.

Resigned, Julia waved back, nodding. With a pronounced lack of enthusiasm, she rose from her desk, and let herself out of the little office.

As she crossed over the little walkway bridge to the main lot, Barb was already moving across the parking lot to meet her. Her expression, however, was not angry – actually, she looked concerned.

"Can I help you?" Julia asked.

"I'm worried about Frank," Barb said. "I haven't heard from him in over two weeks."

Julia nodded.

"He said he was going out of town."

Barb frowned.

"The last time I talked to him, he told me he'd signed our divorce papers. And he sounded pretty down about it."

Barb shook her head – the mannerism of someone afraid she was recognizing something she'd seen before.

"Frank has been known to 'howl at the moon'. He's also prone to mood swings."

Barb eyed Julia seriously.

"So, I'm wondering if he didn't sink a little too low this time."

Julia frowned, remembering his evasive language – leaving town – might be gone a while. She glanced over at Frank's truck, and its two-week coating of dust.

Signing divorce papers could be seen as a settling-of-affairs – the sort of thing you do right before you end it all.

"Okay," Julia agreed.

She turned and stepped back quickly into the office, coming out a moment later with Frank's room-key. "Let's go take a look."

As they walked together back across the lot, the windows in Frank's apartment seemed to blink. It was a bit breezy, and the curtains billowed as if from an open window somewhere in the house.

Julia's arms dotted with a flush of gooseflesh. She

squeezed Frank's room-key, wondering what they might be about to see.

Most likely, it was just an empty apartment, she assured herself. Frank was just on an extended camping trip – a drinking binge over finalizing his divorce.

But Julia still found her heart hammering as she fitted the key into the lock.

She glanced at Barb, whose own eyes were grim, as if bracing herself.

Julia turned the key and pushed open the door.

Cautiously, tentatively, they stepped inside.

And found themselves looking at an empty apartment.

The lights were off, but the kitchen window was open, letting in the sun. That was where the breeze was coming from.

It was odd, Julia thought. It had been over two weeks since Frank left, but the place lacked the musty, empty feel of an unoccupied dwelling. There was a humidifier pumping, and the heat was set surprisingly warm.

Barb looked on the kitchen table.

"Well, damn," she said. "Here they are. My papers. He *did* sign them. He just never put them in the mail."

Julia looked around the empty place.

"You think he just forgot?"

Barb shrugged.

"Sometimes he drinks. All bets are sort of off, then."

Barb turned, perusing the room, as if looking for something she wasn't seeing. Then she focused briefly on the sofa – blankets still twisted on top.

With her face a deepening frown, Barb turned

towards the bedroom. The door was half closed and she pushed it the rest of the way open.

There was light from within, like a grow-light – or a sunlamp.

Barb stopped cold, standing stone-still at the door.

"Oh my God," she breathed.

Julia chilled at the sound of her voice.

Was Frank in there? Had he hung himself? Or shot himself? Or...?

Julia couldn't bear to finish the thought. Instead, she simply braced herself, and looked over Barb's shoulder into the room.

The room was empty except for a large glass... well, what *was* it exactly?

A terrarium? It took up more than half the floor, in place of a queen-sized bed.

It was mounted with a sunlamp, and had a bubbling pool at one end.

The top lid was standing open.

Barb was looking around warily.

"Be careful," she warned. "Stay away from the dark corners. And any large furniture."

Julia was wide-eyed.

"What's wrong? What was in that thing?"

Barb held up her hand, as she bent to inspect what looked like a large dust-mouse on the floor – it was twisted with bits of hair.

And car-keys.

"*Oh my God,*" Barb said again, and this time her voice broke in a half-tearful choke. "*...Frank...*"

Julia shook her head.

"What? What is that?"

Barb stood back, taking Julia by the shoulder and pulling them both urgently back and out of the room.

"It's python shit," Barb said.

Julia blinked, not sure she'd heard correctly.
Barb nodded grimly.
"We need to call the police."

CHAPTER 18

While they waited for the police, Barb told Julia all about Frank's pet monster-snake.

Julia found herself nodding numbly, connecting a lot of unpleasant dots, as Barb told it all a second time to Officer Hamilton when he arrived with yet another cadre of emergency vehicles.

Barb also showed them a series of pictures – Frank and Buffy, through the years. A record of her growth-cycle.

Julia gaped at the size of this *'pet'*. All this time, it had been right there, in that *little* cage.

Except, apparently, for when it had gotten out.

No one had said so yet, but that could account for a lot of things.

One of them might just be Eleanor's missing dog.

The old lady was standing at her door, watching the police activity. Julia had talked to her briefly, explaining in a few words.

She deliberately didn't mention her little dog, although Eleanor was obviously thinking it.

And *everyone* was thinking Lila's name, but no one had spoken it out loud yet, not even Officer Hamilton.

But the cops had brought in a big team from the city, hoping to go over Frank's place with a forensic eye. There was the caveat, however, that doing so might put them face-to-face with a giant man-eating python.

So today, they also brought a local reptile expert, who worked as caretaker of the reptile enclosures at the Denver city zoo – a rather mild-looking middle-aged fellow named Phillips, who was not enthusiastic at the prospect of meeting Buffy firsthand.

When he found out they were dealing with a snake over seven-meters, he shook his head, pulling his phone from his pocket.

"This is out of my league," he said. "I'm no python specialist. I'm a veterinarian for reptiles."

Phillips tapped a number.

"I'm calling the Venom-One hotline. It's a paramedical unit that specializes in cases of exotic snake-envenomation. They're based out of Florida, but they network across the entire country, and can locate the best sources of anti-venom locally.

"They are also," he added, "snake wranglers. And coming from Florida, with all the invasive Burmese and African rock pythons, they're used to dealing with big constrictors."

An operator answered, quickly and briefly, "This is the Venom-One hotline. Please describe your emergency."

"I'm just outside of Boulder Colorado," Phillips said, putting the call on speaker. "I've got a twenty-four-foot man-eating python on the loose, and I need help catching it."

There was a brief pause.

"I have several numbers for you to call," the operator said. "Have you tried the local zoo in Denver?"

"I'm actually the reptile keeper there," Phillips replied. "But this is more than I can handle."

"Understood. We have people here that can help you, but there is also a reptile-house at the Los

Angeles Zoo that keeps big constrictors. Jerry Larson is the local-guy there. He's closer. If you want, I can give you his number."

Phillips took the contact information, thanking the operator.

"If Jerry can't do it, call us back," she said. "We can fly someone out there tomorrow."

Phillips thanked her again and hung-up, turning to the others.

"Well," he said, "let's look at the apartment. Make sure the thing isn't still coiled-up in there, somewhere."

Hamilton shrugged at Officer Miller, who nodded to the empty apartment.

"You go first," Miller said, not joking.

"I actually don't think she's in there," Barb said. "It's a pretty small place. And she's pretty damn big."

"There was also a window open," Julia added.

Barb nodded to Hamilton.

"But you can still go first," she said.

"Thanks a lot," Hamilton replied, unenthusiastically, stepping warily back inside the apartment. Phillips followed, perked like a cat as he looked around.

Barb was right. There really weren't many places to hide. Once they looked under the sofa, that was basically the whole living room. The entryway closet door was already half-open, and the floor was clearly visible, as well as a few of Frank's jackets – there was nothing that could hide a twenty-four-foot python.

The bedroom, where the cage was kept, was a little sketchier. There was a walk-in closet, with a couple of Frank's old military uniforms hanging, and the floor was packed with storage boxes and camping gear. But once they'd pushed it all around, there was nothing there.

Frank had lived pretty lean. If Buffy was in there, it would be hard not to see her.

Barb showed Phillips and Officer Hamilton the left-over snake-feces lying on the bedroom floor – still with Frank's car-keys wrapped in the middle like inside a spider's silk.

Phillips gathered the specimen up, keys and all, dropping it into a plastic container.

"Snake feces contain hair," he said. "Pieces of bone. That would likely contain DNA evidence of its last meal."

"The car-keys aren't enough?" Barb asked.

"There was also that little girl," Phillips reminded her.

Barb turned, regarding the other piles of snake-shit – some still in the cage. The vet was probably right. Lila was likely in one of them.

Phillips scraped several pieces of snake-dung out of the cage.

"She's a big one, alright," he allowed. "I've never seen reptile-scat this size."

"I told you," Barb said. "Frank thought she was a world-record."

"Well," Phillips said, "in order to digest a hundred-and-eighty-pound man in less than two weeks, it would have to be a snake well over three-hundred-pounds."

"Buffy hit three-hundred-pounds *years* ago," Barb said. "It was a milestone. Frank threw her a party."

Barb shut her eyes, shuddering at the memory.

"He bought her a live pig. A special dinner."

"That wasn't a warning signal?" Officer Hamilton asked.

"It was," Barb returned, shortly. "We were divorcing."

She glanced at the papers on the kitchen table.

"That's why I came over here," she said. "He signed the papers. Made it official."

She stopped, breath catching briefly.

"It was probably the last thing he did," she finished.

And then, as she thought it, the realization of it – the *reality* of it – all hit her at once.

She was suddenly struck by grief – for her marriage, her *husband* – for Frank.

Abruptly, Barb began to cry – tears of regret – of horror at how he died – outrage.

Hamilton said nothing. Julia put a hand on her shoulder, but Barb pulled away, accepting no comfort, turning away until it all came out.

It took a couple of minutes.

When she was finished, she looked at the others apologetically.

"I'm sorry. I guess that was coming."

Phillips had stepped out of the room, taking a call. Now he poked his head back in.

"That was Jerry Larson. He said he'll be here tomorrow."

Barb wiped the remaining tears from her eyes.

"He better bring a friend."

"He told me he was bringing a team. Said they'd wrangle it up no problem."

"Unfortunately," Hamilton said, "that's still tomorrow. For now, that thing is still on the loose. It's fortunate that, except for this particular complex, this isn't a populated area, but people still need to be informed. Folks around will need to keep their kids and pets inside until we find it."

And with that, he motioned Barb and Julia outside, as Officer Miller began cordoning-off the doorway – bright yellow tape, just like Darcy's apartment across the lot, marking Frank's apartment a crime scene.

CHAPTER 19

Buffy watched all the proceedings from the pond. She'd spent most of the day lounging after nabbing Eleanor's dog. The unfortunate pooch had been sniffing interestedly by the water's edge, no doubt intrigued by Buffy's own reptile smell.

The little dog had barely gotten out a single squawking bark before he was wrapped and hauled into the water. The attack was so quick, there was less of a splash than when one of the ducks flapped across the surface. It would have been within Julia's field of view from The Glen's main office, if she'd been looking.

In point of fact, Julia, sitting at her desk, *had* glanced over absently at the movement, and turned back to her screen, thinking nothing of it.

Buffy swallowed the dog underwater, and since then, she'd hovered just below the waterline, her beady eyes poking out like a crocodile, invisible on a surface covered in lily-pads, and forest debris from the surrounding trees.

She'd also sampled one of the ducks, which she grabbed from below while it was floating on the surface. The pond was proving to be a fruitful hunting ground/hideout.

The water was, however, a little on the chilly side. In the summer, it would warm up quickly, but right now, Buffy was missing her sunlamp.

There was, however, a lot of activity going on in

her apartment.

Primitive animals like Buffy don't exactly think, but they perceive the world around them just fine. The posture of the hominids running around the lot carried the air of a threat, and so Buffy simply stayed out of sight, not venturing out of the water until most of the activity in the lot had cleared away.

But there were still police in her apartment, locking the place up.

And so Buffy had gone over to Eleanor's place.

She was still hungry, and followed the scent of the remaining dog, right up through Eleanor's little makeshift doggie-door – the one she had insisted Frank install for her – the one she was a tad-bit neglectful about keeping locked.

Buffy poked around the entrance until her nose hit the switch. There was the doorbell sound that Eleanor thought was so cute and quaint, and the latch on the door unlocked.

The opening was barely two-feet wide, but Buffy was able to get in just fine.

When Eleanor came hobbling in, responding to the brief, strangled bark in the kitchen, she found her little dog already being constricted.

If she'd just walked-in on the snake by itself, Eleanor certainly would have fled – assuming she didn't just drop with a heart-attack – but with her pet in the clutches of this... *thing*... the old lady grabbed a cutlery knife and waded-in, hacking away.

Unfortunately, the creature's coils were like steel, and it seemed utterly unbothered at being cut or stabbed.

Her little dog's eyes had gone wide, like a balloon blown too full, right at the point of popping – it was no longer barking, or even struggling.

Eleanor turned the knife to Buffy's head, chopping behind the neck where its jaws had latched on.

This got more of a reaction. The teeth let go of the dog and latched onto Eleanor's arm.

It wrapped her in less than a second.

The old lady weighed barely a hundred-pounds. Buffy squeezed her heart stopped inside thirty-seconds.

But the coils still held fast for another ten minutes – long enough to guarantee brain-death.

Buffy never even entirely let go of the dog, which had gone quiet and still, but the big python now discarded the furry little ball in favor of the larger meal.

Eleanor was slightly built, so her narrow shoulders were less of an issue, but Buffy knew this style of prey now. Without fumbling, she flipped the old lady on her side, coiling and twisting her head against her shoulders, just as she had done with Frank.

Once her prey was positioned comfortably, Buffy began to swallow, crawling her jaws vertically over the old-lady's twisted shoulders.

She went a lot faster than Frank. In five-minutes, Eleanor was gone.

CHAPTER 20

It was several days before Julia realized what was missing – Eleanor's barking dogs.

The Glen had already seemed pretty desolate over the past week. Julia had received notices from four tenants canceling their leases – all the young couples.

So far, there had been no sign of Frank's snake.

That expert from the LA zoo, Jerry Larson – a thirty-something guy, who asked her to call him Jerry – had been out checking the place. He actually seemed excited. Catching a three-hundred-pound python was like a working holiday.

He brought a pair of interns with him, both post-grad herp-specialists, a young man and woman, who introduced as Bob and Lisa, and matched Jerry's recreational air.

Officer Hamilton showed them both the grounds and Frank's apartment. Jerry was particularly impressed with Frank's terrarium set-up.

"Pretty deluxe for the snake," he remarked approvingly. "Space-efficient but roomy. The sunlamp is a nice touch."

He also raved over the pictures he was shown – the shots of Frank and Buffy that Barb had turned over to the police.

"Oh, she *is* a beautiful girl."

Julia had eyed him oddly, and almost reminded him this '*beautiful girl*' had probably killed and eaten two people, including a young child.

But she stayed quiet, simply leading them around the property.

"The good thing," Jerry said, critiquing the layout, "is that this is a pretty basic, minimal complex. Square-block buildings surrounded by pavement. There's not a lot of places for a snake to hide, if you're just walking through the parking lot."

Then he had pointed to the pond.

"That's the bad news," he said. "She could be hiding in there. If it was a little warmer, later in the year, I'd say it was a good bet."

But he shook his head, turning to indicate the surrounding woods.

"Unfortunately," he said, "the water's probably a bit cold for her taste right now. My best guess is she's out there in the brush somewhere, probably holed-up under a dead-log or some burrow."

Now he looked worried.

"If that's the case, we better find her soon, or she'll probably die. It's too cold this time of year. More importantly, too cloudy."

"I'm actually a little more concerned about the safety of my remaining tenants," Julia said.

Jerry nodded. He'd given the property a once-over for snake-proofing. The place had seen repairs, but it had a solid, accessible foundation, and a search under each individual building turned-up nothing. Windows were not cracked, doors were not loose. Jerry laughed when he saw Eleanor's steel-mesh security-screen door.

"No snake is getting through *that*."

Jerry gave Julia his direct number.

"I think you should be fine. But you *do* need to keep an eye out. Everyone who lives or operates around here should be very careful. Especially around the forest's edge, or the pond. Pythons are ambush hunters. Kids should definitely not be outside unsupervised."

"There aren't any kids," Julia replied. "Not anymore."

That dimmed Jerry's cheerful manner slightly.

"Right. Well, pets need to be careful too. Cats and dogs should be kept indoors."

He tapped his card as he handed it to her.

"Call me for anything."

Julia nodded neutrally.

The troop of them had been back by the property twice, scouting the surrounding trees for tracks or signs – perhaps more droppings – but nothing turned up.

Julia dutifully posted warnings on all the remaining tenants' doors. The entire parking lot was empty. Four tenants were already moving out, and the rest seemed to have abandoned the place – most of the other cars were gone.

The warning notice was explanatory and brief, instructing everyone to be careful and watch their pets.

She didn't mention kids.

And not that many of them had pets anyway – a couple of indoor cats, and the only dogs were Eleanor's.

Dog, Julia corrected. One had gone missing.

That was when it occurred to her, she hadn't heard any annoying barking for the last couple of days.

Julia wondered if Eleanor had joined the rest of the tenants and gone to stay with friends or relatives. Eleanor was chatty – she'd mentioned daughters and sisters, so she could have gone off with them.

Although, if she had, someone must have come and gotten her, because her old Cadillac was still in its spot.

Julia frowned doubtfully. She tended to watch the old lady's apartment, and hadn't seen anybody come to pick her up.

Just like Frank had never been picked-up either.

The unwilling picture painted itself.

On impulse, Julia grabbed the key for Eleanor's room.

The empty lot was eerily still as she crossed over the little footbridge. The pond below was like a mirror – she could see her watery twin looking up at her out of the water.

Be careful near the pond, Jerry told her.

Julia shuddered.

There was no answer when she knocked on Eleanor's door. Nor was there any barking.

That might be a good sign. If she'd gone to stay with family, the old lady would definitely have taken her dogs with her. And if something had happened to her, with the dogs – *dog* – in the apartment, you would think the pooch would be yapping its head off.

Julia considered. She wasn't legally allowed to just poke around a tenant's apartment without notice. She'd already done it once this week, and wasn't happy with what she'd found.

"Oh, what the hell," she muttered, and turned the key in the lock, pushing the door open.

"Eleanor?" Julia called softly. "Are you in here? Are you alright?"

There was no answer.

Like the parking lot, the apartment was still.

Julia stepped in gingerly, looking around. The lights were on in both the living room and the kitchen.

The TV was on, but the sound was off.

The living room was undisturbed. There was a coffee cup on the end table, with a spoon in it, and Julia could see the Mr. Coffee on the kitchen counter percolating on automatic.

Then her eye caught a little furry bundle curled up on the kitchen floor.

It was Eleanor's dog.

Julia bent to the lifeless ball of fur – its skin was room temperature. It had been dead for a few days, and was beginning to stiffen up.

There were no obvious injuries – the little dog was just dead.

Julia stood, looking around the apartment warily.

Watch dark corners, she thought.

Then her eyes turned to the sliding glass door and the dog-door inserted into it. She remembered when Frank had installed it – against his better wishes, as she recalled.

"Oh *no*," Julia whispered.

She quickly turned for the front door, nearly tripping over the coffee table, knocking over the half-full cup and spilling it onto the floor.

Reflexively, she bent to pick it up.

As she did so, she realized that the couch beside her was mounted on ten-inch legs, with flaps of fabric hanging around the side, hiding the space underneath.

Julia pulled back quickly.

Eleanor had an old walking cane propped against the door, and Julia grabbed it up, cautiously using it to pull back the flaps, and look under the couch.

It was dark, but she could see nothing there. She pulled back the other side.

Still nothing.

Holding onto the cane self-consciously, gripping it

like a club, Julia stepped back, looking around the empty apartment.

Whatever happened to that dog had been at least a few days ago.

Right about the time the police and Jerry's team had been fruitlessly searching the grounds.

Julia didn't know where Buffy had gotten off to now, but had a good idea where she'd been hiding out then.

As for Eleanor...? Julia was morbidly certain the old lady wasn't staying with sisters or daughters.

Repressing a shudder as she glanced back at the dead dog, Julia turned for the door, pulling out her phone and tapping up the police yet again – Officer Hamilton's direct number this time.

She paused, waiting for the ring.

Movement behind her caused her to jump.

Her breath let out, as she saw it was just billowing shadows from the kitchen curtains.

Nevertheless, her skin was breaking into gooseflesh, and Julia turned back quickly for the door, scooting back outside with a shiver, pulling the door firmly shut.

And in the apartment behind her, the movement she *hadn't* seen, was followed by a disgruntled *thump*, as Buffy, who had been sidling out from under Eleanor's bed, skulking up behind Julia as she tapped on her phone, now turned away, stymied.

The big python nosed briefly at the dead dog, which had gone stiff and unappetizing.

Then she turned to the doggie-door, nosing along the opening until she found the switch.

There was the sound of a doorbell as she let herself back outside.

CHAPTER 21

Buffy lay for a little while in the brief sun-break. The day was still overcast, but at the moment, the clouds had broken up and the UV rays came through unfettered.

Weighing over three-hundred pounds, Buffy had a degree of mass endothermy, meaning that it took a long time for her large body to cool. She could therefore tolerate cold weather. The flip-side was that she conversely took a while to warm up, and she needed core-heat.

Eleanor's apartment was comfortably warm, but Buffy's reptile-brain instinctively understood that one intruding hominid usually meant there would be more of them. That was the pattern, and patterns were something a predator was tuned to recognize.

She also knew that eliminating that first invader would sometimes keep them from coming back with the rest. So when she'd started to move on Julia, it had been more a territorial thing, rather than hunger.

Buffy had swallowed Eleanor six-days ago, and while the old lady was mostly digested, the big python was not really hungry yet. That was to say, she was not actively hunting.

That was *not* to say she wouldn't have been happy to eat Julia too, had she managed to nab her.

But for the moment, Buffy was more interested in body-heat. With the sun peeking through the clouds, the big snake stretched-out luxuriously along the edge of the pond, absorbing the sunbeams while they were there.

There were no neighbors to see her.

And while she would have been in full-view from the office window, Julia happened to be away from her desk, standing in the parking lot, in *front* of Eleanor's apartment, waiting for the police.

It was only when the scraping of gravel and the vibration of tires on the road above signaled the arrival of emergency vehicles, that Buffy slithered off her perch.

A fairly simple creature, Buffy's first instinct was always to get out of sight.

But she also remained perked with interest. Her movement after Julia had initiated the attack sequence, and with that having been aborted, she was still agitated.

She was also eyeing these roving hominids that pattered about a lot more speculatively, lot more *purposefully* now.

Not that reticulated pythons weren't already enthusiastic generalists when it came to almost *any* prey they could fit down their gullets, but Buffy was becoming a specialist. Being an extremely *large* snake, meant she needed high-calorie returns.

The ducks in the pond were plump and meaty, but only bite-sized. It was the same with the small population of carp.

These house-apes, on the other hand, were hefty enough to fill all her calorie needs, without having to go root around in that cold pond.

Right now, however, the police were rolling down into The Glen's main lot – that meant too many of them.

The big python convulsed briefly as she started to move.

It was a bowel movement, ejecting the last little scraps that were left of Eleanor out onto the bank.

Buffy slid into the pond.

Now she was starting to feel hungry again.

CHAPTER 22

The Glen's parking lot was yet again a crime scene, with more flashing lights, but this time there were no neighbors standing around to watch.

Julia wondered at what point the damned place actually qualified as unhallowed ground. She was starting to get the creeps just being out there alone.

The four couples who'd broken their leases were already gone, presumably staying with friends, or possibly even having moved into their new residence. Of the two tenants who *hadn't* given notice, two of them were the traveling businessmen, who weren't home much. That left the two working-Joes, who paid rent, and slept there. Right now, both their cars were gone. Julia assumed they were staying in the city, probably with girlfriends.

Today, Julia was the only one waiting when the police arrived.

Officer Hamilton frowned grimly when Julia showed him Eleanor's dead dog.

"Just to be thorough," he said, "there's no possibility the old lady might have wandered off, is there? Did she have any signs of dementia?"

Julia shook her head.

"No. She was very sharp. Just little and old."

Jerry's team was back, searching the grounds, and going through Eleanor's apartment.

Bob the intern had discovered Eleanor's doggie-door.

Jerry had shaken his head regretfully. He'd actually remarked on the steel-mesh screen the conveniently-sized aperture was built so decoratively into.

"Well, it sure *would* have kept that snake out."

Julia remembered Frank confiding to her that the biggest flaw in the design was that Eleanor didn't always keep it locked – evidenced by both her dogs often running around loose.

Or at least they used to.

Lisa the intern had bent over the dead dog in the kitchen, searching for tell-tale signs.

"Look," she said, pointing to several abrasions on the neck. "These are bite-marks." Then she indicated splashes of blood and the cutlery knife on the floor. "It looks like someone put up a fight."

"It must have come in here after the dog," Jerry said. "It looks like it's been wrapped. I'm guessing the old lady walked in and tried to stop it."

Julia shut her eyes, picturing Eleanor rushing in to save her little dog, literally attacking a giant, man-eating python with a knife.

While searching the grounds outside, however, Jerry found grim evidence of how that struggle ended – more signs – another lump of hair and finger-nails wrapped in a dust-mouse of snake-scat, right near the edge of the pond.

Jerry nodded to Bob, who bent to scrape the specimen into a glass container.

"We'll run the DNA tests," Jerry said, nodding to Officer Hamilton, "but I think you can call that pretty conclusive circumstantial evidence."

Then he turned out to the pond.

"And now, I'm guessing your culprit is right out there somewhere," he said. "So the next step is to start going through that pond."

Hamilton had called in a paramedic-team with search-and-rescue equipment, but when Jerry asked about scuba-gear, the medic expressed reluctance over fishing around in the pond after a giant man-eating snake.

The medic, a young guy, who seemed new on the job, shook his head doubtfully.

"I'm not exactly trained for this sort of thing."

"Don't worry," Jerry said promptly, his manner reverting back to his enthusiastic, recreational air, "*I* am."

He grabbed-up a face-mask and snorkel, and pulled the scuba-tank over his shirt and shorts.

Then he held up a four-foot metal snake-hook, smiling as he wielded it like a sword.

"I'm just going to prod her along a bit."

"What if it goes after you?" the medic asked.

Jerry indicated his team.

"We wrestle big constrictors all the time," he said. "It's our job. A snake this size is a handful, for sure, but there are three of us. My biggest worry is I might get bit before I see her."

He waved the snake-hook.

"That's what this is for. If she's hiding, I just need to poke her out, and get her up to the surface."

He nodded to Julia, who was shaking her head involuntarily just at the thought.

"How deep is this pond?" Jerry asked.

Julia shrugged.

"Five feet or so, throughout most of it. Maybe six or seven-feet at the deepest spots."

Jerry nodded agreeably, pulling on his face-mask.

The Glen kept a little boat for maintenance-purposes. Jerry instructed Bob and Lisa to paddle along the surface above him, as he poked along the bottom.

They spent two-hours combing the fifty-yard pond. Jerry moved methodically, prodding each loose branch and piece of vegetation, covering every square foot with the probing hook, the boat staying just above his trail of bubbles.

He finally came up, sputtering, climbing out the other side, pulling off his mask, and throwing off the air-tank. Discouraged and disappointed, Jerry looked back out on the water.

"Well," he said. "It ain't there."

As he began to peel off the scuba-gear, Jerry nodded to the woods.

"That means she's probably hiding in the brush somewhere," he said. "Pythons, especially retics, can blend into the foliage like big chameleons. She could be hiding five-feet into the bushes and you wouldn't see her."

Another hour, however, searching with dogs turned nothing up.

Stymied, Jerry threw up his hands.

"I don't know what to say. It's gotten off somewhere."

He eyed Julia meaningfully.

"You need to be careful."

Julia shuddered. Right now, she might be the only person still living here at The Glen. If she stayed the night, she would be the only living person within miles.

She began to wonder if that was being stupid. But it was both her job and her home, and she didn't really have anyone local she could stay with. Her family was all out of state.

Officer Hamilton gave Frank's apartment a final

once-over before leaving.

He looked through each room, checking under the furniture and in cabinets. The main closet was standing open. The walk-in closet in the bedroom was an empty floor with a few of Frank's army uniforms lined along the back – all open and visible.

All empty.

"You've got my direct number," he said to Julia, handing her back Frank's room-key. "Call any hour of the day."

Hamilton glanced around at the empty complex.

"Are you going to be alright, out here alone?"

Julia wasn't entirely sure, but nodded.

She closed Frank's front door and locked it behind them.

The police and Jerry's team were another few minutes gathering up, and then the troop of official vehicles pulled in a procession up the steep driveway, leaving the lot empty, except for Eleanor's old caddy and Julia's own little eco-rig. Frank's truck had been impounded, as possible evidence.

Standing there alone, the only sound was the highway – a steady background roar, like the ocean at the beach. Julia used to find it comforting – lulling.

Now it sounded desolate – deserted – like the wind blowing through an old ghost town.

It was the sort of sound that might hide other sounds. Stealthy sounds.

Julia shivered, turning back to her office. She might just close up early today. As in, right now.

Then something caught her eye.

There was movement in Frank's window – the flip of a curtain.

They had closed the open window. Julia had seen each room searched.

It was just the odd flick of a curtain. Nothing more. There was no need to go check it out.

Deliberately, she turned back towards the office.

And behind her, the curtain fluttered again – and a gust going through the apartment was really all that it was.

The breeze was coming through the walk-in closet in the bedroom.

Behind Frank's uniforms, cut right into the wall, was an access-door leading out under the building, as well as up into the roof.

This was actually how Buffy had gotten out before, not the kitchen window.

The opening was loosely covered with a plywood door, painted to match the wall, but mounted on a hinge – rather like a doggie-door. The latch that sealed it had been broken away years ago.

Frank never even realized it was there – it appeared as simply a depression in the wall, perhaps a hole that had been repaired – it wasn't like there weren't several other spots with similar patch-jobs throughout the entire place. The complex was at least two-decades old.

But Buffy had found it, nosing it out – in just the same way she seemed to know when her cage was unlocked.

Besides being a convenient and unobtrusive avenue underneath the building and outside, it was also a nice little hiding place all by itself.

Just a little while earlier, as Officer Hamilton prodded through the hanging clothes, Buffy had been waiting patiently, just on the other side of the thin plywood, for him and all the other intrusive hominids to leave.

When they were finally gone, she slid her full

length back into the room.

Her cage was waiting – the water-pump still going, the sunlamp warm and toasty – the lid still standing open.

Buffy climbed up over the rail, settling in, coiling up for a hot-tub, a sunbath. She would lounge in luxury until hunger coaxed her out once again.

CHAPTER 23

Barb saw Buffy had made the news again. That local anchor-girl, 'Alissa Willis', was back on, her expression almost theatrically grave.

"Like something out of a nightmare," she read in somber monotone, "a giant monster-snake is now believed to have killed *and* eaten, at least three human beings. At last report, this creature was still on the loose, and has remained elusive despite hours-long efforts by authorities to hunt it down."

The station cut to live video of the authorities searching the pond. Barb recognized the two interns floating a small boat, with someone in scuba-gear bubbling below.

Barb had shaken her head, thinking that diver couldn't possibly know what he was poking at in five-feet of water.

She shook her head again, realizing she was wrong – it was, in fact, that expert they'd brought in – Jerry Larson.

In Barb's opinion, that was even worse – because he was the one who should have known better.

Frank once said that you could only handle a snake like Buffy if she let you.

He'd said this while stretching her out across the living-room of his small apartment. That had been when they were dating. Barb had been watching from the door, refusing to come in.

Not with the way that snake looked at her – always a little too happy to see her.

Barb believed Jerry Larson was underestimating Buffy big-time.

She doubted Buffy was in a mood to *allow* herself to be handled.

But the search of the pond ultimately turned-up nothing, and the TV cut to an interview with Jerry himself, expressing concern that they find their snake soon.

"For the snake's sake as well as people," Jerry emphasized. "Pythons aren't adapted for this temperate environment. I'm worried that, if we don't find her soon, it means she's dead somewhere out in the nearby woods. And if animals drag her carcass off, we may never know."

The station then switched back to Alissa Willis in her anchor-spot, introducing her own-narrated piece on Frank, himself.

The script gave dutiful attention to his military service, followed by a series of mostly positive recollections from his neighbors and acquaintances.

There were only a few who knew anything about his pet snake. There were a couple of his army buddies. Barb recognized Randy, the primary culprit and co-conspirator in most of Frank's latter-day drinking forays.

"He raised that python from a hatchling," Randy told the camera. "He took care of it like it was a kid."

Randy had shaken his head, his normal, jovial manner subdued. He was another military man, who'd seen his share of violent death, but Barb could see the brief shudder.

She was still having moments like that herself.

Her husband had been identified by DNA in snake-shit. Barb got the confirmation from the police just that morning.

She had been settling Frank's affairs. Her lawyer told her to hold-off on filing the divorce papers Frank had signed. If need be, they would be binding by the date, should there be concern over any possible liability as his wife.

At the same time, without filing, all mutual assets would revert immediately to her as his legal spouse – it might make things simpler.

In the meantime, Barb had arranged for a funeral service. Frank's parents were dead, his military buddies were scattered – mostly he saw them when they just showed-up, blowing through town. She'd given the service-date two-weeks lead-time, for just a small ceremony at a local veteran's church, where Frank would be given a plaque.

There was no body.

Trying not to think too much about *that*, she wondered instead who might be there to pay respects?

Herself? Maybe Randy, or the Jones brothers?

A few old acquaintances, who perhaps cared enough to feel a bit bad about his passing.

Barb wondered if she would cry. She would try not to. She'd done a lot of that in the last week. Frustration, anger, disgust.

While the part of her that grieved didn't want to think about it, she realized that, after the little girl was taken, Frank must have known.

Buffy would have... had a lump.

Barb remembered that crack she'd made about his snake eating that kid.

Frank's response had been just right – deflecting quickly, but not quite denying, which would have been suspect.

Barb, of course, had been an easy sell – she'd *thought* it, but didn't believe it.

Rephrase that – she very much didn't *want* to believe it.

And so she hadn't said anything either.

Barb paused a moment on that.

If she'd spoken up after that little girl had disappeared, at least two more people, including Frank, himself, wouldn't have been eaten by that snake.

And Darcy certainly wouldn't have shot Eddie.

Barb wondered what weight that gave her to bear.

She decided she'd acted in good faith. She hadn't really believed it, or she *would* have said something.

And she had also been trying not to be over-cautious and get Frank in trouble – that was her trying to be nice.

That's what *that'll* getcha.

She'd gotten the call this morning that her lawyers had decided she should file for divorce after all, citing less possibility of attachment to any liability should survivors decide to pursue damages. All the rights of a widow should still apply, but it was best to be separate from Frank Walker's affairs going forward.

Barb would not deny that – she'd already been getting calls from the local news, and the story was gruesome enough to possibly go national. The last thing Barb wanted was to remain Mrs. Frank Walker.

Best to be Barbara Jordan again.

And so her last act as his wife was to end their marriage, even after he was dead. It seemed ghoulish.

It might also be irrelevant, as she realized she didn't have Frank's signed papers. She couldn't find them anywhere.

After tearing her files apart, she stopped,

remembering.

They had been on the kitchen table at Frank's apartment.

She'd been just a *bit* distracted that day. She must have left them there.

Cursing, Barb picked up her phone and pulled up Julia's number.

CHAPTER 24

Hamilton was on his way home when his partner called from the station.

The Glen's jurisdiction was within the city of Boulder, and Miller had been working on most of the Darcy Chapman-shooting part of the investigation from the downtown station. And since he was already at his desk, he'd also taken the opportunity to do some background searches on the property.

The complex's current owner was an investment company that had picked up the property after the original builder/owner filed for bankruptcy, and then subsequently died. Miller had called the utilities companies, looking for blueprints, as well as a topical map of the surrounding terrain.

He was looking for possible cubbyholes, or tunnels for piping, built into the hillside, that might fit a twenty-four-foot python.

What rang the cherries, however, was a little different.

"What'cha got?" Hamilton asked when Miller called.

"Well," Miller replied, "it turns out unit 12, Frank Walker's apartment, was originally the onsite caretaker's place. The old utilities room used to attach to the back. It was torn down when the city-inspectors demanded his power-network for the complex be upgraded. That's the expense that drove him bankrupt. The new utilities room was built into the main office, when the new owners remodeled, and unit 12 was given new siding and a roof. But there's still a crawlspace in the back of that big walk-in closet, and it leads both up onto the roof and under the building."

Hamilton's heart kicked up a notch. Now everything made sense.

They'd looked under the foundations of each building – Jerry and his team, moving carefully with snake-hooks and bright lights in the cramped space, as well as scouting for escape routes or loose gratings.

But they hadn't thought to look for built-over passageways.

When the dogs had searched the grounds, they found just the two trails – one from Frank's apartment to the pond, and the other from the pond to the old lady's house.

The paths were both ways.

"That's it," Hamilton said. "It's gotta be. That thing was getting in and out through the crawlspace. It was probably hiding in there while we were searching the apartment."

"That's what I'm betting," Miller agreed.

"Gotta go," Hamilton said, ending the call.

He tapped Julia's number. The line rang until it went to voicemail.

Hamilton frowned. He left a message at Julia's prompt, and also sent her a text.

Then he tapped-up Jerry Larson's number, even as he hit the lights on his cruiser, pulling a U-turn, turning back towards the highway and The Glen apartments.

CHAPTER 25

Julia was watching the televised coverage of her day when her phone rang.   She frowned when she saw Barb's number, but picked up the phone.

"This really is not a good time," she said.

"I saw," Barb replied. "It's all over the news."

Right now, the TV was showing Alissa Willis' interview with 'veteran Officer Bradley Hamilton', who looked uncomfortable in front of the camera, and was the very definition of *'just-the-facts-ma'am'* as he detailed the day's events.

"Based on evidence collected around the scene, we believe that the missing tenant is deceased, and that our escaped python was responsible. DNA analysis will confirm this in the next few days."

A fairly delicate way of saying they'd found Eleanor's hair, fingernails, and a couple of pieces of jewelry in a pile of snake-feces by the pond.

Julia also happened to be privy to another update that Hamilton was not yet sharing with Alissa Willis.

The DNA evidence had come in on both Frank and the little girl.

"I have to call Darcy Chapman first," Hamilton had confided to Julia. "I don't want her to hear it on the news."

He had taken a breath, forcing himself to say it.

"I have to tell her Lila was eaten by a snake."

And Julia knew the deeper ramifications of that statement. Up to now, the police had mostly kept mum on the implications concerning Lila. Hamilton had offered no further comment on any of Alissa Willis' questions in that direction.

Because of that, the public conversation had not yet drawn the obvious conclusion.

If the snake did it, that meant the guy Darcy *shot* did not.

"Will it affect her legal case?" Julia asked.

Hamilton had shrugged. "You never know. It shouldn't. It's still self-defense against a violent boyfriend with a restraining order who escaped from jail."

But he sighed.

"On the other hand, it does change his motive for being there. It also begs the question of whether she would have shot him otherwise."

So far, Alissa Willis' news report hadn't mentioned Darcy Chapman.

The TV switched from Officer Hamilton to footage of Jerry Larson searching the pond, followed by a brief interview with him and his team.

"Special experts," Alissa Willis intoned, "who are here today putting their very lives on the line."

Jerry had raised an eyebrow, glancing at Lisa and Bob.

"Don't get me wrong," he said into the microphone, "no one should try this at home. Like anything that carries risk, it requires training.

"But the good news," he emphasized, "is we aren't dealing with a horror-monster, or a serial killer. This is just an animal acting on its instincts.

"Of course, the bad news," he added dutifully, "is that still makes it a predator large enough to see humans as prey. So anyone in the general area should be watchful. I don't want to overstate the danger.

Snakes don't travel that fast. It's highly unlikely there is any risk to the public more than a mile or so in any direction. And that's at the very outside. I actually expect to find her holed-up somewhere within a few hundred yards of this complex. And if she's out there more than a couple weeks, we'll probably find her dead."

Jerry smiled at the camera reassuringly.

"So the danger is low. Only people living very close really even need to worry."

Which, Julia thought dismally, would pretty much just be *her*.

At this point, the idea of spending the night out here, completely alone, left her on edge. She was beginning to think a motel might be better. She had a credit-card that she kept for things like car-repairs. It had a low limit and a few night's lodging would max her out – she also realized it would mostly be for her own comfort-level.

But the thought of listening to the creaks of the building and hoots in the woods once it got dark? And all that covering up what you *really* needed to hear, which was stealthy and subtle – a knocked-over vase as a loose window was nudged aside, allowing *just* enough space...

When Barb called, Julia jumped – the startlingly loud ring-tone injected another mocha-shot of adrenaline into her already strung-out system.

Still, she tried to be patient. Barb was one of the bereaved, after all. So Julia listened. Social-worker 101.

"I've been settling Frank's affairs," Barb explained. "But I need the papers Frank signed, and I think I left them in his apartment. You know... *that* day." She cleared her voice. "They should still be there. Would you mind letting me in?"

Julia glanced over across the lot. Frank's window curtain was fluttering again.

"It's a crime-scene," Julia said. "No one's supposed to cross the barrier."

"I know," Barb said. "But I just want to be done with this. You've got the key. Can you just help me out?"

Julia shuddered at the thought of going back into that place even one more time, but she sighed.

"I'll run over and get your papers," she said reluctantly.

"Great," Barb responded. "Thanks. I'm on my way over right now."

The phone beeped off, and Julia set it down, grabbing up the key for unit 12.

Across the lot, Frank's apartment sat waiting quietly – just as dead and empty as every other building in the complex.

Kinda had a '*Bates Motel*' sort of feel to it.

Julia shivered again.

She glanced furtively over the railing, as she crossed the little foot-bridge over the murky, glassy pond. Jerry Larson's team had searched every square foot – it should be safe. But Julia kept deliberately to the center of the narrow walkway, her eyes wary to either side.

Her heartbeat ticked-up a notch as she stepped up to Frank's door, pulling the yellow police tape aside, and fitting the key in the lock. In the dead stillness, there was a startlingly loud 'click' as she turned the latch and pushed the door open.

They had left the lights on inside. Neither had they turned off the heat. Frank kept the apartment warm, which Julia now realized was probably him accommodating his pet snake. Briefly putting on her manager-hat, she found the thermostat on the wall and turned it down. She also would have to remember to cancel Frank's electric service and terminate his lease.

She switched off the hallway and living-room lights, but there was still illumination coming from the bedroom. The sunlamp on Buffy's snake-cage remained on – Julia could hear the water-pump still running.

Turning, she was about to move to the bedroom, when she spotted Barb's papers, still sitting on the kitchen table.

As she walked past the bedroom door, partially ajar, she did not see Buffy coiled unobtrusively in her cage, her camouflaged pattern blending even with the minimal artificial foliage.

Julia bent to examine the papers on the table.

Then a hint of movement behind caused her to turn.

Standing in the kitchen, she now had a more direct view of the bedroom through the half-open door.

Buffy was propped-up out of her tank, reared like a cobra. The python's head was leveled exactly at Julia's own five-foot-seven.

The serpent's eyes were yellow and unblinking. Julia always heard how snakes could hypnotize prey – like Kaa in *The Jungle Book*.

She could almost believe it, because she stood frozen for a vital second – paralyzed by those eyes.

They were blank – like a doll's eyes – but something in that eager stare was almost gleeful.

Happy to see you.

But not in a good way.

Julia's eyes cut to the front door, which she'd left standing open. She measured the distance.

The room was fourteen-feet wide. Buffy was more than twenty-four-feet long – and unlike Anacondas or the more bulky Burmese pythons, that length came with deceptive agility. Reticulated pythons chased monkeys right up into the trees, their elongated bodies circling around the trunks like unwinding fishing line.

Buffy came streaking out of that tank like greased spaghetti.

Julia screamed and bolted for the door.

The apartment complex was empty and dead – there was no one to hear her for miles around.

She screamed anyway – guttural, hysterical, and completely involuntarily.

Her hand latched on the front door knob, just as she felt needle teeth latch onto her thigh.

Julia was pulled down, and then she felt the heavy weight of the coils – three-hundred pounds of writhing steel.

It wrapped her in less than a second.

Julia's wind came out in a single agonized gasp – one last lingering cry.

"Somebody HELP ME!"

Then the coils constricted and she had no more breath to scream.

CHAPTER 26

Barb was beginning to get an unwilling sense of what Frank's last days must have been like.

As she pulled out onto Interstate 25, leading out towards The Glen, a number of unpleasant dots were connecting in her head, and they formed an ugly picture.

Frank was out of town the weekend Lila disappeared. But if the snake had gotten out, and then back in, he would *had* to have known what happened – it would have been obvious.

That would explain his sudden change of heart – finally signing her papers – settling his affairs.

Barb knew about the incident years ago with his neighbor's cat. Frank had told the story to her like penance.

What might have been his reaction this time to come home and find Buffy with her tell-tale child-sized lump?

Was Frank contemplating suicide?

That would not be out of his character. Not over something like this.

He had obviously chosen to cover-up the actual incident – but she could see how he would have justified it. He *wasn't* 'getting away with it' – he just didn't want anyone to know.

It was all about penance. Just like with the old lady's cat – except this debt had required much more than that single pound of flesh – and it had been collected without spilling a single drop of blood.

For a moment, Barb's eyes stung with tears, because she saw a small bit of the Frank she'd loved – in the midst of this sordid awful mess, that was a desperate attempt to find some sense of nobility.

Barb knew the shame he would have felt – how he would have judged himself – a little too little, a little too late.

For her part, Barb wasn't sure how she felt about it yet.

Definitely, not good.

Frank, after all, had chosen the snake.

Barb shook away the blink of tears, as she turned onto the access-road that led to The Glen apartments. Another half-a-mile and she turned into the nearly empty parking lot, down into the gully.

As she parked in front of the small foot-bridge, Barb could see through the office window that Julia was not at her desk.

Barb parked her car, peering in through the glass.

There was a small TV playing on the desk, where Julia had been watching the news. The programming had moved past Buffy on to traffic.

Barb turned, looking back at Frank's apartment.

His truck was gone – impounded. The apartment itself was still cordoned off with straps of tape marked 'crime-scene'.

But Barb saw the tape on the front entrance was pushed aside and the door was standing half-open.

Julia was obviously fetching the papers.

Not particularly wanting to go back into the place herself, Barb waited by her car for Julia to come out. But several minutes passed and no one appeared at the door.

Maybe Julia was having trouble finding the papers. Barb hoped the police hadn't grabbed them up for some reason. Or possibly moved them – last she recalled, they were lying on the kitchen table.

After another couple minutes, Barb finally started across the parking lot.

The complex was utterly dead. The rest of the neighbors had apparently abandoned the place.

Barb couldn't exactly blame them. The news coverage had been sensationalist and gore-crow, as the press was by nature, despite Jerry Larson's pacifying comments.

Truthfully, despite the tragedy, and her own grief, Barb knew the general threat was low, and she wasn't personally afraid. She had, after all, lived with Buffy for almost two-years, and the snake mostly just sat in its cage.

Despite the bite wounds on her leg, Barb knew a python wasn't going to come running out of the woods, and chase you, like a tiger. It was about the nature of the beast and knowing the perimeters of risk.

Out on a highly visible parking lot, with room to move, she should be safe enough.

The creeps she was feeling were likely just from the general bad vibes that had permeated the place over the last few weeks.

Still, she was dutifully cautious as she pushed the door to Frank's apartment the rest of the way open.

The living room was quiet. The kitchen light was on. There was light coming from the bedroom.

Barb stepped into the apartment, looking around, watching for possible movement in every corner.

"Julia?" she called out, her own voice sounding loud, as she stood in the deliberate stillness.

There was no answer.

Barb poked her head into the bedroom, feeling a little breeze as she did so, although none of the windows seemed to be open.

The light was coming from the sunlamp on Buffy's cage. It was still on, the pump on the pool still motoring softly.

Barb stepped back to the main room, and now she spotted her papers still sitting, right where she'd left them on the kitchen table.

Relieved, she took a half-step that way, when the front door suddenly slammed shut from a gust of wind.

Barb screeched, her heart jumping, pumping a dose of adrenaline into her system.

She let her breath out. The wind gust came out of the bedroom. Maybe an open vent?

Barb turned back to the kitchen, grabbing up her papers.

Then she noticed the room key also still sitting on the table – a manager's copy.

Frowning, Barb pulled out her phone and dialed Julia's number.

There was an immediate ringtone coming from the bedroom.

Slowly, cautiously, Barb followed the ring.

She found the phone lying on the floor, just inside the bedroom door. Her own number blinked up at her.

Then she heard shuffling in the walk-in closet.

Her heart thudding like a drum, Barb turned to look.

There was slithering movement. With her blood turning suddenly to ice, Barb realized there was going to be something there to see.

Buffy was flopping on the floor, her whole twenty-four-foot body writhing spasmodically.

Julia's legs were sticking out of her throat.

Barb stood frozen, much like Julia herself had, rooted in utter horror.

For a moment, she felt the impulse to run in and help – to grab onto Julia's legs, and try and pull her out of the python's gullet.

But she knew how impossible that would be – just pulling your hand out of its teeth would be like dragging your skin through a tangle of barbed-wire.

It would also already be a wasted gesture. Barb knew pythons didn't swallow their prey while it was still alive.

As it turned out, it would also be redundant. Buffy *wasn't* swallowing Julia – the snake was puking her back up.

Constrictors – snakes in general – were known to regurgitate meals when threatened, making themselves lighter, and more able to either fight or escape.

Barb now saw the open panel on the wall, where Frank's hanging uniforms had been pushed aside. She felt the breeze coming from within.

An access-way, Barb realized.

Buffy had been trying to get through the small space, but couldn't fit with Julia still inside her.

Now, cornered and threatened, the big snake vomited her last meal out onto the hardwood floor. Julia's head bounced like a loose bowling ball as Buffy spat the last of her out. The young woman's eyes were open – bugged-out and dead – the expression on her face was surprised.

Already, her skin was clammy and pale.

Barb suppressed her own gag-reflex.

Buffy pushed away from her forfeited meal, her massive coils twisting rapidly, as she moved into the next phase of the territorial threat response.

The big python's head cocked – its eyes turned and locked on Barb's own.

Freezing. Hypnotizing.
Happy to see you.
But not in a good way.

CHAPTER 27

Even as Barb stood there in physical paralysis, a whole constellation of dots were now connecting in her head.

No wonder they hadn't found it. It had simply come right back in. Then they'd locked the place up, left her water-pump running, sunlamp on and the thermostat set to tropical.

And now here she was – her gut freshly-vacated, her twenty-four-foot body poised like an arrow, coiling behind her for the spring – then going suddenly still as her eyes locked on their target.

In that frozen time-lapse pause, Barb remembered how it was those same beady yellow eyes that she'd never gotten over – that first-glance, identifying her as potential prey – the 'predator's eyes', Frank called them.

And Barb had felt that unwavering stare every single day she'd lived with Buffy – a predator, focused and watching for its chance, with literally nothing else on its peanut-sized mind. After a while, it felt almost like a personal grudge.

It was utterly amoral – implacable.

Relentless. Sly.

And inhumanly patient – Buffy had literally waited years, until that opportunity came – that last day Barb had lived with Frank, when it had almost gotten her.

Now here it was again.

Did it recognize her? Perhaps by scent? Maybe even by sight?

Did it *know* her?

Have you been waiting for me, Buffy? All this time?

Barb had gotten that *look* from her from the very first moment they met.

Had it been a threat response? Perhaps a territorial thing, or even a rivalry of some sort over Frank?

Or maybe it was not even that deep. It might be that Buffy just simply saw her as a mouthful, no different than anything that happened to walk by, capable of fitting down her distended gullet.

After all, a snake was almost *always* looking for something to eat. Outside of mating season, if it was moving, that was why.

"There are two kinds of animals," Frank once told her, with his typical wry grin. "Snakes. And snake-food."

And Buffy, who had a *big* appetite, had just puked out her last meal.

Lean and limber once again, she attacked.

The big python lurched forward, teeth-first, springing like a Jack-in-the-Box, launching three-quarters of its length, eight feet out the closet door, with the rest of her already coiling behind her for the next strike.

Barb stumbled backwards into the bedroom, barking her hip sharply on the cage, nearly falling, but catching herself and circling behind it.

Buffy's first grab fell short, but she was coming forward purposefully. The four-foot high cage sitting in the way was not much of an obstacle – reticulated pythons scaled trees in seconds – she would slide right up over the top.

Barb glanced at the door. If she could circle around a couple more steps, she would have a straight shot.

But Buffy was in stalking mode, moving more deliberately now after the first missed strike. Her nearly foot-long head remained arrowed unerringly in Barb's direction, even as she coiled-up in the small room like a giant rattler, loading-up the spring for another attack.

The moment the prey moved, was when the strike would come. That was actually where the myth of snakes hypnotizing prey came from – rodents would often sit stone-still when confronted at close-quarters by a predatory serpent, so as not to give themselves away.

Of course, that was an extremely short-term strategy – the stand-off would only last until the snake got close enough to bite.

Buffy's head popped up on the other side of the tank, right in front of the open lid. Barb stood motionless as that frozen rodent, even as those yellow eyes found her.

Buffy paused over the opening.

Barb stayed stone-still.

But the giant python seemed to have paused.

The cage, Barb realized, was Buffy's doghouse. It was *her* place, somewhere she felt safe. If this was all because she felt threatened, it was possible she might go back in on her own.

For a moment, Barb almost dared hope.

"*Go on,*" she whispered, even though she knew snakes were deaf and Buffy couldn't hear.

The big snake nosed around the opening, even as her coils followed her up on top of the tank.

Then her tongue flicked, tasting the air, and her head arrowed back at Barb.

"Oh *shit!*" Barb blurted, and bolted for the door.

She made it three steps before the teeth snagged

her leg – the same damned spot, right over the old scars.

Except this time she knew there would be no one showing up to rescue her. They were in a secluded gully, half-a-mile off a major Interstate – she could scream all day.

Barb screamed anyway, yanking her leg away before the teeth sank deep enough to grip – she felt her skin tear, but her leg pulled free.

It was, however, enough to trip her up. She fell lengthwise, landing hard, losing her breath. The living-room was now cut off. Gasping, she turned to the walk-in closet – a possible refuge, but when she had fallen, she had knocked the door shut.

Buffy was already coming at her again.

Still sucking back her air, Barb made another leap for the living-room.

This time, she felt the impact of teeth almost immediately – the weight of the blow was like getting slugged by a heavyweight fighter, striking her in the shoulder, the impact knocking her down once again.

It would have been over right then except Buffy's jaws latched onto Barb's purse, with only a couple of the needle teeth catching her shirt and the flesh below.

Barb rolled on the floor, wrenching loose, throwing her purse off her arm, choking out involuntary screams as she lost a little more skin, and more of her own blood splattered her face.

On her hands and knees now, Barb lunged for the apartment's front door.

Buffy spat out the purse without coiling and came again.

Barb screamed as the teeth caught her leg – the same leg, already bleeding, but now the teeth sank deep.

It had her this time.

The instant the grip was sure, the coils came.

"*Noooooo...*"

Barb's voice cracked as she fought desperately, but she had no chance at all.

In less than a second, Buffy wrapped.

Barb struggled on her knees into the living-room before toppling on her side, with three-hundred-plus pounds bearing her down. The python's coils wrapped her leg, twice around her waist and chest, and once between her neck and shoulder.

The pressure was like being in a full-body blood-pressure-cuff, that just kept pumping tighter. Barb's breath gasped out in a last effort to scream, barely managing a hoarse whisper. It seemed as if her very skin might burst, or her eyes pop out of her head.

Barb couldn't blink, but as her consciousness began to flicker, the world dimmed.

As she began to fade away, a passive, half-removed part of her mind marveled at how easy it was.

In about seven minutes, she would be brain-dead.

Buffy would hold her a bit longer just to make sure.

And when Barb was transformed into a dead piece of meat, Buffy would swallow her, just as she had Julia.

Call it fifteen minutes, start to finish.

Barb's last breath gasped out as Buffy tightened her coils.

The world faded to black.

There was a crashing sound and a sense of falling.

Then there was a voice.

"Oh my God! Get *off* of her!"

Barb blinked back awake at the sound of another slam, which she now realized was the front door.

Officer Hamilton was standing there. His hand

was on his gun, but he looked torn as to where to shoot. Instead, he just simply leaped on top of them, wrestling for Buffy's head.

Barb could have told him how to get the snake to release – she remembered Frank used alcohol, but probably any nasty-tasting caustic liquid would do. There was also very hot or very cold water, or you could bend the constrictor's tail. All those would work.

Unfortunately, Barb couldn't speak. She couldn't even move her arms to point. And in another few seconds, she was going to black-out again.

Realizing he couldn't pull the coils away, Hamilton had his baton out, and was trying to wedge it into the snake's mouth. Barb could feel her skin tear as he tried to pry the teeth loose.

As if for spite, the coils squeezed tighter around her.

Buffy's tail swatted Hamilton's face. Reflexively, he stomped the tip with one foot.

And for a miracle, Barb felt the constrictor let-go – a stomp was apparently as good as a bend.

But Buffy clearly didn't like it. Even as Barb felt the coils fall away from her chest, and the teeth disengage from her leg, she saw the giant python twist and strike back at her antagonist.

Hamilton staggered backwards, trying to dodge, but the jaws latched onto his face, digging like fish-hooks into his neck and cheeks.

The coils came less than a second later.

Hamilton choked out a pig-like squeal of agony, as his face was torn, spurting blood, and then he toppled over backwards with Buffy's full weight on top of him.

He went down with both arms trapped and three coils around his chest – the python's fangs were buried deep into the flesh of his cheeks and scalp.

Barb rolled onto the hardwood floor, suddenly free. Disoriented and light-headed, she climbed to her knees. Blinking herself back to awareness, she turned to see Hamilton about to die in Buffy's coils.

It was already close to too-late.

Barb was still gasping for breath, and her body felt brutalized, like she'd just been rolled under a car, but she staggered to her feet, stumbling for the kitchen.

She threw open the cupboards, rummaging quickly – tempted to grab the bottle of bleach, except that Buffy's teeth were latched onto Hamilton's face, Barb instead grabbed a fifth of tequila.

It was one of three. Barb reflected briefly that Frank only had multiple bottles on hand after coming *off* a binge – '*going on the wagon*', he called it, which meant drying out for a few weeks or months.

That was also suggestive of his final days – cold sober. That would have been part of the attrition, not allowing himself the balm of the bottle.

Too little. Too late.

Barb cracked the seal, turning to where Frank's pet monster was killing Officer Hamilton.

If it hadn't already.

Still staggering, Barb nearly fell on top of them as she poured the tequila over Hamilton's face and Buffy's jaws.

The alcohol vapors burned Barb's own nostrils as she poured the whole bottle down the snake's gullet, recalling old memories of bars and parties, shots and lemons, followed by hours of retching and morning hangovers. Barb's own stomach convulsed with nausea just at the memory.

Buffy didn't like it much either. The effect was instantaneous – the snake released, her jaws dropping loose from Hamilton's face, and the coils fell off him like loose clothes, as the big python went slithering away like a banished garter snake under a rock. Barb could see its head thrashing back-and-forth, like a dog spitting out a foul taste.

The snake was retreating for the bedroom – it was after the access-way, but their struggles had slammed the closet door shut.

So instead, Buffy turned and climbed back into her tank. Her full twenty-four-foot length slid up and over the side in a blink, through the open lid, and she coiled herself down into the deepest part of her little pool.

Cautiously, Barb followed her into the bedroom.

Buffy watched her through the glass cage – her head was underwater, making her yellow eyes appear large and bulbous. The snake's mouth flexed, as if chewing, still rejecting the taste of tequila.

Barb walked over and shut the tank's lid.

Deliberately, she set the latch.

That was apparently all that was wrong with it.

Buffy was a captive once again.

The yellow eyes betrayed no emotion as they stared at Barb through the window. The hypnosis-thing seemed to work even through the glass.

Perhaps there was a baleful lilt to those dead, unblinking orbs.

You got away again, they said.

Barb wrenched her gaze away, turning back to where Officer Hamilton lay on the living-room floor.

CHAPTER 28

Hamilton groaned painfully, holding his face, as he started to sit up.

"Oh, *Jesus*," he breathed, struggling to regain his wind.

Barb bent beside him, holding him down. He was bleeding badly. One of the teeth had nearly punctured his right eye. The rest of his face was a jigsaw of deep, ragged cuts, that would be difficult to stitch, and would leave nasty scars.

But better that than the alternative. It had been very close.

"Sit still," Barb said, as she turned back quickly to the kitchen for towels and a pail of hot water. Then she set about doctoring Hamilton's face. The fabric where she daubed him quickly became soaked red.

"I'm okay," Hamilton said, even though he clearly wasn't, but he sat up deliberately, taking the red-stained towel himself, holding it to his face as he looked around for Buffy. "Where did it go?"

Barb pointed to the bedroom.

The door was ajar, and Buffy sat complacently in her cage, still submerged in her little hot-tub, soaking away the taste of tequila.

Hamilton eyed the big snake purposefully. Brushing Barb's restraining hands aside, he stood.

With one hand still holding the towel to his torn, bloody face, the other reached for the gun on his hip, pulling it from its holster.

Barb stepped after him, holding his arm.

"Wait. What are you doing?"

Hamilton cocked his pistol.

"What do you think I'm doing?"

Barb shook her head.

'No. She's trapped."

"That's a dangerous animal," Hamilton said. "It's killed people. It needs to be put down."

"You'll get no argument from me," Barb replied. "But let the professionals do it. If you open the cage to shoot it, it's not trapped anymore. The brain is the only sure kill-spot with a bullet." Barb held her fingers a peanut-width apart. "*That* size a target. And good luck hitting it through all those coils."

She pointed to Buffy's head, which was currently still submerged at the bottom of the tub, the rest of her body coiled on top of her. Trying to shoot her head from the cage-lid would be impossible.

Hamilton pulled the bloody towel away briefly, looking down at the red stains, and then back at the snake-cage.

"The '*experts*' might not put it down," he said.

Barb didn't say anything. But she understood him just fine.

In her head, she knew it wasn't personal – Buffy was just an animal – and that peanut-sized brain meant there were no higher emotions guiding her actions.

At least, that was the science Frank always quoted.

But sometimes Barb wondered if the basic ones weren't enough. Reptiles showed both anger and fear. Combined with recognition and memory, that might be mental-ingredients enough for a long-term grudge.

And frankly, at this point, she didn't care if it was personal to the damn snake or not.

It was to *her*.

Barb wanted that goddamn thing dead.

Maybe it was wrong to hate an animal – petty, perhaps – it might even be leftover jealousy because her husband chose it over her.

Fine, she granted it all. She hated the damn thing anyway.

And Hamilton was very likely correct – if the experts were Jerry Larson and his crew, they certainly would *not* put it down.

Barb could already see Jerry raving about what a beautiful girl Buffy was.

She tensed but didn't object as Hamilton stepped up in front of the tank, kneeling down right beside it – right where Buffy still coiled in the pool, with her head underwater.

Hamilton put the barrel of his pistol up against the glass, aimed directly between the python's eyes.

Those beady yellow eyes.

Buffy never lost a stare-down – she didn't even have eyelids to blink.

And that predatory glint was as eager as ever.

There was no doubt what would happen if there was no glass between them.

Barb still dreamed of those beady, ever-staring eyes.

As happy to see you as ever – and never in a good way.

But today, Officer Hamilton stared right back at her, eye-to-eye.

And *definitely* not in a good way.

He aimed the gun carefully. To Barb's eye, at that range, he should be able to hit the target.

Still, the glass might vary the shot slightly. And that might be all it needed.

And then there would be broken glass, and an

angry, shot python that was no longer caged.

Hamilton stepped back, holstering his pistol, turning away with clear reluctance.

Buffy reacted not at all.

"Larson's already on his way," Hamilton said, disgruntled. "We'll let the experts handle it."

He pulled out his phone, wincing as he reflexively touched it to his torn face. Tapping the screen, he tossed it to Barb.

"Here," he said. "Call for an ambulance."

Behind them, Buffy lay coiled, still comfortably submerged, relaxing in the bubbles of the filter-pump, as she watched the two hominids in the other room.

And that gaze remained a bit more *purposeful* than before.

It was not just that reticulated pythons weren't already happily notorious opportunistic predators, nor was it even her recent conditioning, learning to specialize according to available prey.

This was the development of a *taste*.

Of course, in the limited way that Buffy understood things, she realized that, right now, at least, she was back in a locked cage.

For the patient predator that she was, that just simply meant it was once again time to wait.

She would be watching with those beady yellow eyes, always staring, never blinking.

And she would be ready when opportunity presented itself next.

Sooner or later, it always did.

CHAPTER 29

Buffy was taken into custody without further incident – or only minor incident.

When Jerry arrived with Lisa and Bob, the big python bit the *shit* out of Jerry's hand. She'd started to coil him too, but the two trained interns got her to release fairly quickly, and between the three of them, they managed to get Buffy packed away into a travel-crate, and loaded onto a police van.

Jerry took a selfie, holding up his injured hand, and the widely-spaced tooth-marks.

Barb and Officer Hamilton were both taken to the hospital. Barb was mostly given a once-over – her own injuries were relatively minor. Buffy's coils left bruising with some skin abrasions, and she might have sprung a rib, but should recover just fine.

Upon her release, the first thing Barb did was give Frank's signed papers to her lawyers. Then, after giving her official statement to the police, she promptly left town. She canceled the lease on her rented house, and went to stay with her sister in Denver. The press had started circling and her lawyers advised her to keep a low profile.

Right now, the story was simply that people had died – horribly. No one had thought to hold anyone responsible – yet – but it was best to keep her public attention minimal.

Officer Hamilton was kept in the hospital overnight. His face was stitched together like a quilt, and the scarring would be extensive. They pulled out a snake-fang embedded in his cheek.

But beyond the scars, and the possibility of a face that looked like a Picasso painting, he was expected to make a full recovery.

The local news jumped on the story, before it broke nationally, with Alyssa Willis appearing on-camera at the hospital, the police station, and even back out at The Glen, which was now an empty lot, cordoned-off at the main-drive with crime-scene tape.

As more details trickled out, the story continued to develop new twists. Darcy Chapman was being sued by Eddie's family, for wrongful death. They were also suing the cops.

Theoretically, Darcy's case for self-defense should still apply – and that remained solid – but she was going to have to go through all the money, lawyers, and bullshit anyway.

When the press asked about the suit against the police, Officer Miller – who was the new public face of the investigation since Officer Hamilton's formerly-handsome mug had been turned into chopped meat – had offered up a stiff "No comment."

Although, Miller told Hamilton privately, he thought the city would end up settling their own suit, and paying Eddie's family off – probably through the nose. They were indulgently generous with tax-payer money, especially if it meant bad publicity.

Hamilton didn't know yet what any of it implied for his own career. He had been in charge of the case, after all. Right now, the lawsuit was aimed at the police department in general, and not *him*, specifically, but he imagined it was only a matter of time before someone singled him out.

And of course, he had been perfectly right about

the snake being spared. To his knowledge, there hadn't even been any discussion about putting Buffy down.

That by itself pissed him off.

Perhaps it was morally wrong to hold a killing grudge against a near-mindless animal.

But, as he looked through his report file, and the pictures of Lila Chapman, Eleanor Perkins, and Julia Wagner, not to mention his own mutilated-face, Hamilton decided he was fine with being wrong.

As the story began breaking nationally, the press-narrative was shaping Frank Walker as the main villain.

Hamilton wasn't sure if *'villain'* applied, but *'responsibility'* was certainly unarguable.

But in Frank's case, at least, it was a debt that had been paid.

In Buffy's case, it looked like she was being made into a celebrity. With all the perks.

She was initially taken to the city zoo, in Denver, but they lacked the specialized facilities to keep really big tropical herps, and so Jerry set about arranging housing. And when it became publicly known that this wasn't just a man-eating python, but probably a world-record size, the offers were not long in coming.

The LA Zoo was the initial front-runner, but was ultimately outbid by a reptile-park out of Florida, called *Gator Glades*, which specialized in big, dangerous reptilian attractions.

After a certain amount of legal wrangling, primarily involving the last wrap-ups of the police investigation, the sale was made final.

The exact amount Gator Glades paid was not made public, but the beneficiary was the city of Boulder, which had seized the snake as illegal property. Barb simply signed over any claim, even though the financial compensation was rumored to be quite significant. Gator Glades had wanted their python.

Barb's lawyers had advised her accepting any money would be akin to taking ownership – i.e. responsibility. She had suggested putting money in a fund for the survivors of the victims, but was advised to let the city handle it.

Of course, the Gator Glades payment would most likely be turned towards paying the lawyers over the lawsuits. The actual payment of damages to the plaintiffs would come from taxes.

Lose-lose, Barb's lawyers assured her. Best to just stay out of the way as best she could.

Jerry Larson stayed involved with Buffy's transfer to Florida, even putting up a bid for a position on the Gator Glades' staff. Having assumed temporary stewardship of Buffy since her capture, he took it upon himself to oversee the animal's security and welfare – as well as providing for general *human* safety until the big python arrived at her new home.

With much fanfare, Buffy was transported to Gator Glades and introduced to the public.

CHAPTER 30

'Buffy the Giant Man-eating Python' immediately proved to be a popular attraction.

And she did, in fact, turn out to be a world-record. The first thing Gator Glades' park management did was have her weighed and measured.

In a public ceremony/coronation, Buffy came in at exactly twenty-four-feet, five-inches, three-hundred-and-twenty pounds.

Her new accommodations were lavish. Jerry Larson insisted she be provided a sunlamp, similar to her old home, as well as a Jacuzzi pool. Her cage was built long, with an artificial branch stretched over the water, designed to allow her to lounge, while displaying her full body-length to the awed public.

So now she lived like an empress, day-after-day, laying there lazily, leisurely, in utter decadent comfort, staring fixedly back at the milling tourists.

It was a purposeful look that never faded. The eyes of a predator – always watching, always waiting, for that moment when the prey *wasn't* on the other side of the glass.

Sooner or later, that moment always came.

Buffy always perked-up most when she saw the children.

Day after day, they pressed up against the display window, bare inches away, staring in at her, fascinated – almost perfectly the size and shape of Macaque monkeys.

Just like little Lila Chambers.
Her fans.
Buffy was *always* happy to see them.
But never in a *good* way.

THE END

Check out other great

Cryptid Novels!

J.H. Moncrieff

RETURN TO DYATLOV PASS

In 1959, nine Russian students set off on a skiing expedition in the Ural Mountains. Their mutilated bodies were discovered weeks later. Their bizarre and unexplained deaths are one of the most enduring true mysteries of our time. Nearly sixty years later, podcast host Nat McPherson ventures into the same mountains with her team, determined to finally solve the mystery of the Dyatlov Pass incident. Her plans are thwarted on the first night, when two trackers from her group are brutally slaughtered. The team's guide, a superstitious man from a neighboring village, blames the killings on yetis, but no one believes him. As members of Nat's team die one by one, she must figure out if there's a murderer in their midst—or something even worse—before history repeats itself and her group becomes another casualty of the infamous Dead Mountain.

Gerry Griffiths

CRYPTID ZOO

As a child, rare and unusual animals, especially cryptid creatures, always fascinated Carter Wilde. Now that he's an eccentric billionaire and runs the largest conglomerate of high-tech companies all over the world, he can finally achieve his wildest dream of building the most incredible theme park ever conceived on the planet... CRYPTID ZOO. Even though there have been apparent problems with the project, Wilde still decides to send some of his marketing employees and their families on a forced vacation to assess the theme park in preparation for Opening Day. Nick Wells and his family are some of those chosen and are about to embark on what will become the most terror-filled weekend of their lives—praying they survive. STEP RIGHT UP AND GET YOUR FREE PASS... TO CRYPTID ZOO

Check out other great

Cryptid Novels!

P.K. Hawkins

THE CRYPTID FILES

Fresh out of the academy with top marks, Agent Bradley Tennyson is expecting to have the pick of cases and investigations throughout the country. So he's shocked when instead he is assigned as the new partner to "The Crag," an agent well past his prime. He thinks the assignment is a punishment. It's anything but.Agent George Crag has been doing this job for far longer than most, and he knows what skeletons his bosses have in the closet and where the bodies are buried. He has pretty much free reign to pick his cases, and he knows exactly which one he wants to use to break in his new young partner: the disappearance and murder of a couple of college kids in a remote mountain town.Tennyson doesn't realize it, but Crag is about to introduce him to a world he never believed existed: The Cryptid Files, a world of strange monsters roaming in the night. Because these murders have been going on for a long time, and evidence is mounting that the murderer may just in fact be the legendary Bigfoot.

Gerry Griffiths

DOWN FROM BEAST MOUNTAIN

A beast with a grudge has come down from the mountain to terrorize the townsfolk of Porterville. The once sleepy town is suddenly wide awake. Sheriff Abel McGuire and game warden Grant Tanner frantically investigate one brutal slaying after another as they follow the blood trail they hope will eventually lead to the monstrous killer. But they better hurry and stop the carnage before the census taker has to come out and change the population sign on the edge of town to ZERO.

Check out other great

Cryptid Novels!

Hunter Shea

LOCH NESS REVENGE

Deep in the murky waters of Loch Ness, the creature known as Nessie has returned. Twins Natalie and Austin McQueen watched in horror as their parents were devoured by the world's most infamous lake monster. Two decades later, it's their turn to hunt the legend. But what lurks in the Loch is not what they expected. Nessie is devouring everything in and around the Loch, and it's not alone. Hell has come to the Scottish Highlands. In a fierce battle between man and monster, the world may never be the same. Praise for THEY RISE : "Outrageous, balls to the wall...made me yearn for 3D glasses and a tub of popcorn, extra butter!" – The Eyes of Madness "A fast-paced, gore-heavy splatter fest of sharksploitation." The Werd "A rocket paced horror story. I enjoyed the hell out of this book." Shotgun Logic Reviews

C.G. Mosley

BAKER COUNTY
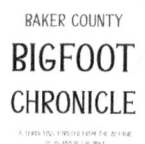
BIGFOOT
CHRONICLE

BAKER COUNTY BIGFOOT CHRONICLE

Marie Bledsoe only wants her missing brother Kurt back. She'll stop at nothing to make it happen and, with the help of Kurt's friend Tony, along with Sheriff Ray Cochran, Marie embarks on a terrifying journey deep into the belly of the mysterious Walker Laboratory to find him. However, what she and her companions find lurking in the laboratory basement is beyond comprehension. There are cryptids from the forest being held captive there and something...else. Enjoy this suspenseful tale from the mind of C.G. Mosley, author of Wood Ape. Welcome back to Baker County, a place where monsters do lurk in the night!